Michael slammed [...]
apartment building's main doors and
pushed them open with force. He was
getting really worked up now.

A cold blast of spring air hit him. The night was dark, even darker than usual. The outside entry light was out. He would probably have to fix it. The land-lord usually took months to fix anything, and this was just plain dangerous.

Michael stepped off the stoop. Out of the corner of his eye, he saw something move. A shape in the darkness. He started to turn toward it when something hit him on the back of the head. The blow was so hard it knocked his teeth together.

"What—?" he asked, but another blow slammed into him, harder than the first.

He saw white, felt his knees buckle. He wanted to turn, to reach whoever was doing this to him, but the darkness had grown worse. He was passing out—and before he had a chance to try to stop it, he toppled forward, into a deep and very painful sleep.

ROSWELL™

Be sure to look for new titles in this suspense series

Available from POCKET BOOKS

Don't miss any books in the original series:

ROSWELL HIGH

Available from POCKET PULSE

ROSWELL™
NO GOOD DEED

Dean Wesley Smith
&
Kristine Kathryn Rusch
From the television series
developed by Jason Katims

POCKET BOOKS
New York London Toronto Sydney Singapore

For information regarding special discounts for bulk purchases,
please contact Simon & Schuster Special Sales at 1-800-456-6798
or business@simonandschuster.com

This book is a work of fiction. Names, characters, places and incidents
are products of the authors' imagination or are used fictitiously. Any
resemblance to actual events or locales or persons, living or dead, is
entirely coincidental.

An *Original* Publication of POCKET BOOKS

POCKET BOOKS, a division of Simon & Schuster, Inc.
1230 Avenue of the Americas, New York, NY 10020

™ & © 2001 Twentieth Century Fox Film Corporation,
Regency Entertainment (USA) Inc. and Monarchy Enterprises B. V.

ISBN: 0-7434-1835-2

First Pocket Books printing September 2001

10   9   8   7   6   5   4   3   2

POCKET and colophon are registered trademarks of
Simon & Schuster, Inc.

Printed in the U.S.A.

For Chris and Steve,
who found the tape

NO GOOD DEED

1

December 24—Phoenix, Arizona

Chad Newcomb removed the cotton mask, scrubs, gloves and paper booties the hospital had made him put on. Then he swept the plastic shower cap from his head, and tossed it all into the recycle bin. He glanced through the glass window that separated him from the isolation area.

Katie lay on the bed, her face so pale and thin that she almost didn't look human. A month ago, she had been a healthy child. A month ago, she had laughed and played and had asked him questions about Christmas.

Do you think Santa will find the new house, Daddy?

Do you think I've been a good girl, Daddy? What if Santa thinks I haven't?

Do you think Santa'll come early this time?

This year, she was too ill to ask if Santa would bring Mommy back. That question had blindsided Chad last

Christmas. His wife Maggie had been dead since January. Katie had been devastated—he had been devastated—but she seemed to get through it.

Mommy's dead; Mommy left but she didn't want to; Mommy was really sick, and had to leave us. None of those answers had worked, so this time, Chad had said, *God took her to live with him.*

Katie's beautiful face, so like Maggie's, had squinched up and turned bright red. *God took her? Tell Him to give her back.*

Chad had had to turn away from his daughter. Her words had captured his feelings so essentially that he had never forgotten them. It wasn't until his parents insisted Katie view the body that Katie had finally understood Mommy was never going to return—or at least he thought she had, until Christmas.

Then the magic of Santa Claus had enticed her. Surely, Santa's magic would give her the present she really wanted—her mother's return.

Chad had done some quick thinking last year to explain why Santa could answer material needs, but not needs of the heart. He had been relieved when Katie had said she understood.

Chad stared through the glass at his daughter. Right now he would give anything to have her ask for her mother again. He wanted to fight the Santa questions, deal with the disappointments and thrills of Christmas, anything—anything, but this.

Katie had been listless and pale for a week before he took her to the local doctor, who had prescribed fluids and bed rest, thinking she had a cold. When she didn't get better, the doctor added a slate of antibiotics, which had done nothing.

A few nights ago, her temperature had spiked to 103, and Chad had brought Katie to the emergency ward. They had stabilized her as best they could, given her tests, and sent her here—the best children's hospital in the Southwest.

The tests, however, were inconclusive, and more were being run. Until then, Katie had to be in isolation. She could have anything, the doctors told Chad. From a serious case of meningitis, to a virus they couldn't identify, to cancer.

Cancer. That word frightened him more than the other diseases. Maggie had died of cancer. Chad wasn't sure he could go through a death like that again, especially that of his—and Maggie's—only child.

Katie was sleeping now, the deep exhausted sleep of the very ill. She hadn't heard him leave. If she stayed true to form, she'd sleep like this for quite a while.

Chad needed a break. A little food, maybe some coffee. Some conversation, someone to share the pain with. His parents were on a year-long cruise, something they had saved their entire lives for, and Maggie had had no family.

He was alone, completely alone.

Chad slipped out of the children's isolation ward. He'd already learned the hospital's rhythms. At this time of night, a single nurse spent much of her time at the desk, reviewing charts and going on hourly rounds. There were other nurses on duty, of course, but the hospital's corridors were mostly empty, accenting the scents of sickness and disinfectant—the feeling of doom.

Children's drawings lined the hallway walls, giving the place a false air of festivity. Some of the drawings were old, and Chad had made the mistake of asking if all of the drawings were done by children currently in the ward.

The nurse who had answered him looked sad. "The children *were* all in the ward," she had said. "Sometimes this is all we have to remember them by."

He looked away from the drawings as he walked past. Katie was too sick to hold a crayon. If she died before the new year, she would never contribute anything to these walls. He wondered if the nurses would remember her at all.

Finally, he saw the bright lights of the nurses' station. Against a nearby wall stood a vending machine where he had already spent too much money. Poinsettias lined the desk, and below the beautiful seasonal plants, someone had strung a row of Christmas lights. Big red bows were pasted to the end of the desk.

The decorations only added to his despair. Children shouldn't be in the hospital at Christmas. No one should.

As he approached the desk, he noted an LPN standing before it, searching through a chart. He had seen her a number of times before. She was short and blond and usually very cheerful. At the moment, though, the pediatrics nurse seemed almost lost. Her head was bent, and he noticed drying blood on the edges of her white nursing shoes.

Another emergency. The place was full of them. How did the staff maintain their balance from day to day? It had to be easier in the regular wards. Adults at least had tasted life.

An intern stood in front of Pediatric Oncology. His scrubs were fresh, not even wrinkled. His dark hair looked wet and was combed away from his face.

He turned toward Chad. Chad got a sense of fear from the man—really, he looked more like a teen. He had the long angular face of a high school-age boy, a handsome face that promised great character as the boy matured.

Surely he was too young to be an intern. But Chad couldn't tell anymore. Since Maggie died, everyone looked young. Young and innocent and untouched by life.

Or maybe he just felt old.

Chad bought a root beer from the vending machine and went to the windows off to the right. The street below was quiet. Only a few cars remained in the parking lot.

Two squad cars sat in front of the emergency area, their lights flashing. How many times a day did the police come here, to bring someone in?

Then he heard the stairway door close, and worried voices echo down the corridor. Chad turned.

The duty nurse, a pretty woman with dark hair and dark eyes, was talking softly to an overweight police officer. Two other officers trailed them, looking worried.

Chad took a step forward.

"I don't recognize him," the duty nurse was saying. Her voice was barely above a whisper, but he still caught the words in the night silence. "He isn't wearing hospital identification. He said he had checked on the children, but he's hovering around the door like he's waiting for someone. I don't like it."

"How long has he been there?" the cop asked.

Chad looked down the hall. The intern was frowning, but he hadn't moved. The boy did look odd. Even Chad had noticed that.

"Apparently I wasn't at the desk when he arrived." The duty nurse rounded the corner. She was walking so fast the cop was having trouble keeping up.

Chad stayed back, standing in the opposite corridor so that he could see what was going on. Why would anyone hover around a door in a children's ward in the middle of the night?

Then he went cold. He didn't like the answers he was coming up with. Neither, apparently, had the duty nurse.

The LPN looked up as the duty nurse and the cops surrounded her.

"If he's a member of the staff—" the cop said.

"He isn't, believe me," she said. "If he were, he'd have something to do."

The intern moved closer to the door, but didn't take his gaze off the duty nurse and the cops. For a moment, Chad thought all they were going to do was stare at each other.

Then the intern knocked on the door, right next to the Pediatric Oncology sign. Three knocks, like a signal.

That, apparently, was enough for the cops. They hurried forward.

The intern pulled open the door and slipped inside. Chad took a step into the hallway, so that he could see even better. The LPN closed her chart and watched.

Chad saw a flutter near the window on the oncology door, and then darkness. Apparently the intern had covered the window with something.

Chad's mouth went dry.

"Oh no," the LPN whispered.

The cops tried the door, but it didn't open. The first cop pressed his considerable weight against it. It still didn't open.

"It's the police!" one of the cops yelled. "Come out of there!"

The frightened duty nurse didn't even shush him, despite the need for quiet on this ward.

"It's the police!"

Chad moved closer. A few of the children in nearby rooms woke up and began to cry out. The LPN went down the corridor, closing doors, her soothing voice mixing with the cops' angry tones.

Two of the cops were throwing themselves against the door now, in a concerted effort to force it open.

"Why in the hell did someone put a lock on this door?" the remaining cop asked the duty nurse.

"There is no lock," she said.

"Then this guy is amazingly strong," the cop said.

"Or he's found a way to block it," one of the other cops said, gasping between words as he continued to throw himself against the door.

"Is there another way in?" the heavyset cop asked the duty nurse.

"No." There was a thread of panic in her voice.

Chad clenched his fists. He hated to feel helpless. He'd been feeling helpless too much lately.

They were on a low floor. Why didn't someone go outside and enter through the window?

The cops continued their efforts. The LPN came

back, watching nervously, her hands clasped before her. Chad glanced over his shoulder, but saw no help coming.

He reached behind the desk, grabbed the metal office chair, and pushed it into the hallway. The sound of chair legs scraping against the floor caught everyone's attention. All five turned in unison to look at him.

He shoved the chair toward them. "Here," he said. "Try this."

One of the cops grabbed it, and slammed it against the door. The door banged open.

The main cop and the duty nurse hurried inside, followed by the other three. Voices filtered into the hallway. Children's voices.

Pattycake, pattycake, baker man.
Bake me a cake as fast as you can...

Chad leaned forward. Except for the children's voices, no one else spoke. There were no sounds of violence. And no one emerged from the room.

The children's voices fell silent.

Chad's heart started to pound. He hurried down the hall and stopped at the door.

The two nurses and two of the cops were still standing there, watching several children jump on a bed. Two young girls were sitting in front of a lit Christmas tree, smiling at the adults. The children were the picture of health.

The heavyset cop stood near an open window, peering outside. The breeze coming through it was icy cold.

"What happened?" Chad asked.

"It's a miracle," the LPN said in a stunned voice. She stared at the children.

Chad frowned.

"All of those children were dying," the duty nurse said slowly.

"Are you sure they're still not?" he asked.

"No more than the rest of us," said the LPN, a smile breaking over her face.

"How can you tell? Don't you have to run tests?"

"Mr. Newcomb," the LPN said, turning to him, "none of those children had enough strength to get out of bed half an hour ago. I wasn't sure if some of them would make it through the night."

He looked at two boys, jumping on the bed, laughing and giggling like normal children.

"What do you think happened?" Chad asked one of the cops.

"I have no idea," the cop said.

"Angels," said a little girl near the Christmas tree. "An angel came and healed me."

She lifted her shirt. A silver handprint covered her small stomach.

Everyone gasped. The duty nurse hurried toward her, touching the spot. "Does it hurt?"

The little girl giggled. "No."

The other children lifted their shirts, revealing similar handprints. They were smiling.

"It's a miracle," the LPN said.

Chad was shaking. *A Christmas miracle? Could it be possible?* He felt, for the first time in days—maybe even in years, a bit of hope thread through him.

Then he turned and ran down the corridor, past the nurses' station and toward the isolation ward. He could hear his own breathing, ragged and hopeful and frightened all at the same time. He was saying Katie's name softly as he pushed the isolation ward door open and looked through the window.

She was still asleep. Her little face wasn't pale anymore. Instead, it was a sickly white-green. He knew with a father's instinct that she was no better. In fact, in the short time he had been gone, she had gotten worse.

"That's not fair," he said brokenly to a God he wasn't sure was listening. "If you were going to heal all the children, why not Katie? Why not my Katie?"

Chad looked through the other windows, his hands clenched at his sides. He saw other sleeping, restless, horribly ill children. No one had saved them, either. If angels had come down from the heavens to heal children, they would have healed all the children, not just a select few.

That intern had looked real. He had been frightened, Chad thought. He had knocked three times—a signal that meant he and someone else had been afraid of being caught.

They had escaped, not by vanishing, but by going through a window.

They were human, and they used some kind of experimental cure on children on Christmas Eve. A cure that left a silver handprint on smooth, young skin.

The cure had to work on all sorts of diseases. Cancer wasn't one thing. It was many things. And just because the children had all been in Pediatric Oncology didn't mean they had the same kind of cancer.

Most of those children had been sicker than Katie—and they had been cured.

Chad grabbed his coat from the chair he had left it on, knocking the book he'd been trying to read earlier to the floor. He slipped the coat on and hurried outside, hoping he could catch what was left of that miracle.

For Katie, as well as for himself.

2

March 23—Roswell, New Mexico

Michael Guerin grabbed the remote, flicked off his TV, and blinked at the sudden darkness. Darkness? How late was it? He leaned across the couch, stabbing his forearm on the spring that was poking out of the cushion, and turned on the light that Max had scrounged for him.

The clock above his ancient stove read 8:15. Michael was late. Worse, he was late to meet Maria.

Michael glanced at his arm. No blood from the spring, just a long red scratch. Someday he would have to fix that couch. Just like he'd have to fix the table he'd found and the stereo, and the VCR.

If only he didn't spend so much time with Maria. Then he'd get some of this stuff done.

He grinned at himself. He liked spending time with Maria. He just hated to do it on a schedule. Check that. He hated to do it on *her* schedule. And everything was on her schedule. He wasn't even sure why they were getting together tonight. He liked just hanging out, but Maria *planned* things.

It would be just his luck that there was a visiting opera company or some fashion show that she expected him to sit through. Her full lips would form a pout and she'd tell him that he'd learn something. Or that he had disappointed her. Or that other boys would go with her.

Michael shook his head and pushed himself off the couch. He was already getting himself worked up. What was wrong with a guy just staying home, eating a take-out pizza and watching the game? How come she didn't join him for that? She would give him that look of hers and say that it didn't sound like fun.

It sounded like fun to him, and if she didn't like it...

He let out a small sigh and shook his head. He was going nuts. Now he was having arguments with Maria without Maria even being present. The girl was stuck in his brain. Oh, she'd be happy to know that he was thinking about her all the time. He didn't want to be, but he was.

Michael grabbed his coat, picked his keys off the crumb-covered kitchen table, and went to the front door. For a moment, he stopped by the phone and stared at it.

Maria would tell him that polite men called when they knew they were going to be late.

But she wasn't his official "girlfriend," and he wasn't polite. She was his former girlfriend, he was late because he lost track of the time, and he didn't care.

Not really. He just had to have all his arguments in place by the time he reached the Crashdown Cafe. No sense in meeting Maria unprepared.

He yanked open the front door to his apartment and took the stairs two at a time, his shoes drumming on the wood. This building always sounded empty, even when people were in it. Which was a good thing, since he and his friends were traipsing in and out at all hours of the night. The last thing he needed was some neighbor complaining to the landlord.

It was tough enough to rent an apartment at his age, pay for it, and keep up in school. It was even tougher when he had to occasionally disappear to deal with alien stuff.

Sometimes he wished he could just be an ordinary guy. In his imagined life, he'd have real parents, like Max and Isabel had, parents who treated him with respect, gave him his own room, and fed him regularly.

Parents who looked at him fondly, even when he made a mistake, just like the Evanses did.

Sometimes Max didn't know how great he had it. Princely Max, who somehow got the best of everything. The great leader. Geez. Even in his past life, Michael was only a general. Not the guy everyone followed. Not the guy everyone admired.

He reached the apartment building's main doors. He wasn't sure what got him going on all of this tonight. Probably being late. Liz would never give Max crap for being late. Of course, Max wouldn't be late, even though Liz wasn't his girlfriend anymore, either. The great and perfect Max would probably have called, just like Michael should have done.

Michael slammed his palms against the doors and pushed them open with a lot of force. He was really getting worked up now. If Maria wanted to go to some dumb

14

play, she was out of luck. They'd have a burger at the Crashdown or go for a walk or something. Nothing planned. He wasn't going to do anything planned.

A cold blast of spring air hit him. The night was dark, even darker than usual. The outside entry light was out. He would probably have to fix it. The landlord usually took months to fix anything, and this was just plain dangerous.

Michael stepped off the stoop. Out of the corner of his eye, he saw something move. A shape in the darkness. He started to turn toward it when something hit him on the back of his head. The blow was so hard that his teeth knocked together.

"What—?" he asked, but another blow slammed into him, harder than the first.

He saw white, felt his knees buckle. He wanted to turn, to reach whoever was doing this to him, but the darkness had grown worse. He was passing out—and before he had a chance to try to stop it, he toppled forward, into a deep and very painful sleep.

Maria flounced into the booth across from Alex. "Do you know where Michael is?"

Alex sopped up a lake's worth of ketchup with a single French fry. He didn't even look up. "It's not my day to watch him."

"Well, it's obviously not mine, either." Maria reached into her purse and took out her mirror. She checked her makeup for the fifth time that hour. The frosted eye shadow hadn't slid into the crease on her eyelid and her mascara hadn't smeared. Her lipstick was coming off, though. She had to stop biting her lips when she was nervous.

And she was nervous. What was keeping him? Something stupid, she would bet. Something so inane as falling asleep on the couch.

Well, she wasn't going to call him. She wasn't going to worry about it at all.

"Do you have something else to say or are you just going to watch me eat?" Alex had been packing away the food since he came back from his foreign exchange trip. He had said he liked the food in Europe, but he had really missed a big greasy burger with a pile of fries. Missed it so much, apparently, that he'd been having it almost every night for supper.

Maria wondered what his folks thought about all of this. Liz's theory was that Alex hadn't really missed the food so much as he had missed Isabel. He spent time in the Crashdown, hoping to see her, and rekindle whatever that weird friendship/moony-eyed thing was that was going on between them.

"Well?" Alex asked.

"Huh?" Maria said.

"Did you want to talk about something?"

"No," she said and slid out of the booth. She went to the counter and stopped beside some guy in a suit. He had a cell phone near his left hand, and a plate of chili in front of him. He looked exhausted.

Liz was making a double-chocolate milkshake. Somehow Maria doubted it was for the guy beside her. It had to be for Alex. Maria waited as the milkshake machine roared. Liz kept her hand on the large metal cup, the little silver antenna on her headband bobbing from the vibration.

The milkshake machine had been out of order lately. If someone didn't hold the cup in place, it would tilt sideways, then splatter all over the wait station. Of course, that had happened to Maria first, in the middle of a busy Sunday afternoon with half the kids from school watching.

Michael had been cooking that day. He'd laughed, and when she challenged him on it, he'd just raised his eyebrows and said, "You really should be more careful."

She had thrown some melting ice cream at him, and missed. That day, not only had she had to clean up the front, she'd had to clean the grill as well. Nothing smelled worse than burning ice cream.

The milkshake machine stopped and Liz turned. "Not here yet, huh?"

She sounded as if she had expected Michael to be late.

"If he were here, would I be?" Maria asked. She rested the arches of her high heels on the metal railing beneath the counter, and leaned forward.

Liz poured the shake into a tall glass, got out the whipped cream and sprayed it into a pyramid on top, leaving off the maraschino cherry. Yep. The shake was for Alex. No one else liked that much whipped cream on a double-chocolate.

"Give me the cherry," Maria said.

"Why?" Liz asked.

"I'm hungry," Maria said.

"Like this is going to make a difference." Liz grabbed a

cherry and handed it to Maria, then put the shake on a tray and walked the whole thing over to Alex.

He was still making a mess with his French fries, and he didn't look up at Liz, either. What was bothering him?

Maria bit the cherry off the stem, leaned over the counter, and threw the stem into a bus tray. As she straightened, she saw that the suit guy was still watching her.

"It's okay," she said. "I work here."

"I know," he said. "You forgot to give me my bill."

"Dang." She got off the railing and hurried behind the counter. She flipped through her ticket book. Sure enough, there was one ticket shoved into the back. The cook had marked his time-out on it, but she hadn't given it to the customer.

Maria slapped it on the counter. "Sorry," she said.

"It's okay. It's not like I have something better to do. This town really rolls up the carpets at night, doesn't it?"

"Actually," she said, "you just have to know where to go. At nine, there's this really great band playing over at the Roadside Inn. There's not a lot of room, though, so you should get there early."

"Fat chance of that," the guy said, glancing at the clock on the wall.

Maria looked too and bit back a curse. "Michael Guerin!"

"What?" Liz said from behind her. "Is he here?"

"No!" Maria leaned against the counter. "And now we're late."

"For what?"

"Remember, I told you we were going to see the Hanging Toenails at the Roadside?"

Liz made a face. "I wish they would change their name."

"They will when some record company discovers them." Maria tapped a red-painted fingernail against her teeth. "I *told* him to get here at eight so we would have plenty of time. I figured we'd get there if I got him moving an hour ahead of time."

"Did you tell him where you were going?" Liz asked.

"Are you kidding?" Maria crossed her arms. "With Michael it's always better to get him there and then tell him. Otherwise, all he'd want to do is sit on the couch and watch football."

"Football season is over," said the guy in the suit.

"What*ever*," Maria said. "Who asked you into this conversation?"

"You did," he said. "We were talking about what to do in this town."

She rolled her eyes and looked at Liz, who shrugged. Liz looked tired. She had a long mustard stain on the shoulder of her blue uniform, and strands of hair poked out of her ponytail.

"Are you sure you didn't tell him?" Liz asked.

"Positive," Maria said. "I know better than to do that."

"Maybe that's why he's not here." Alex's voice carried across the nearly empty restaurant. "Maybe if you'd trusted him enough to tell him what you wanted him to do, he would have been on time."

"And how well do you know Michael Guerin?" Maria asked.

Alex leaned back. "Well enough to know if he really wanted to go to something, he'd be on time."

Maria stalked around the counter toward Alex's booth. "Are you saying he doesn't want to be with me?"

Alex's eyes widened. "Um, no. I didn't say that."

"Well, he's not here, and he was supposed to be here at eight."

"But he didn't know why he was supposed to be here." Alex's voice got a little weaker, as if he knew his argument was on poor footing.

"He knew he was supposed to come see me."

"But he also knew you were working, right?" Alex glanced at Liz. Liz shrugged and turned away, as if she didn't want to be involved.

"So?" Maria asked.

"So you can't always get off on time. He probably figured time wasn't a major factor."

"He always figures time isn't a major factor," Maria said. Then she sighed. "I have no idea why I put myself in this position."

"Maybe you should call him," said the guy in the suit.

"What?" Maria looked at him.

"He's late. Maybe something held him up. Maybe you should call him."

"If something held him up, then he should call me," Maria said.

"And if he fell asleep on the couch?" the guy asked.

"I'll kill him," Maria said.

"Oh." The guy looked toward Alex's booth. "I don't suppose you're still my waitress."

"Do I look like a waitress?" Maria asked.

"I don't know how to answer that," the guy in the

suit said, "since you were my waitress not an hour ago."

Maria let out a huge sigh and sat on one of the counter stools. "No, I am not still your waitress."

"What would you like?" Liz asked.

"Whatever he's having," the guy in the suit said, pointing at Alex's shake. "Only with the cherry and less whipped cream."

"You got it." Liz went behind the counter and started to scoop chocolate ice cream.

Maria drummed her fingers on the tiled surface. "I don't think I should call him."

"I know," Liz said.

"Because if he doesn't care enough to be on time, then why should I chase after him?"

"I wouldn't call that chasing...."

"Then what would you call it?" Maria asked.

"Checking?"

"Oh, good," Maria said. "Michael would really like it if I were checking up on him."

"Isn't that what you want to do?" Liz asked.

"Of course that's what I want to do, but I'm not going to do it because that would be exactly what he expects, and I'm not going to do what he expects."

"Like you're not doing that now," Alex said.

"What does that mean?" Maria swiveled the chair to face him.

"Whenever he's late, you get into some kind of snit. He expects it, so he stalls even though he knows that the longer he waits, the more upset you'll be. Then when he does get here, he's already on the defensive because he knows you'll be mad, and you *are* mad, so you're doing what he expects, and then you spend all your time fighting instead of whatever else it is you do."

Maria stared at him for a long moment. That was just too accurate and she wasn't sure how she wanted to respond. How she should respond.

"Maybe that's just how they relate to each other," Liz said, before Maria could think of a suitable answer.

"Of course that's how they relate to each other," Alex said. "But I'm really tired of listening to them complain about it."

"Michael complains about me?" Maria asked.

"Weren't you listening?" Alex said.

"This does not sound like a good relationship," said the guy in the suit.

"Who asked you?" Maria snapped.

The suit guy shook his head. He wasn't that old, really. It was just his clothing that made him look older. He probably wasn't more than twenty-two.

"Where's my shake?" he asked Liz.

"Coming right up." Liz added chocolate milk to the ice cream, and went back to the shake machine.

"For your information," Maria said, "it is a good relationship."

The suit guy looked over at her, surprised, as if he hadn't expected her to talk to him again.

"Except that you're not having one right now," Alex said.

"One what?" Maria was losing track of this conversation. She glanced at the clock. It was one minute later than the last time she looked.

"A relationship."

"What?"

"I thought you and Michael broke up."

Maria waved a manicured hand. She'd worked hard on that after the shift and now Michael wasn't here to appreciate it. "Technically."

"Technically?" the guy in the suit asked.

"It doesn't really matter because we still go out," Maria said.

The suit guy shook his head. "Does your friend consider it going out?"

"What?" Maria asked.

"Well, if he doesn't consider this a date, he can't be standing you up, now can he?"

Maria frowned. "How come men are always on the same side?"

"Maybe because we speak the same language," Alex mumbled.

"He bought me pearls," Maria said.

"What?" said the guy in the suit.

"For Christmas. He bought me pearls. Now does a guy do that when he's not in a relationship?"

Liz set the shake down on the counter. The suit guy grabbed it like it was a lifeline.

"Maybe you should call him," Liz said.

Maria sighed. "I thought you at least would understand."

"I do," Liz said. "But you wanted to see the Hanging Toenails. If you want to go with Michael..."

"Tell you what," Maria said. "Screw Michael. I want something to eat. A junior cheeseburger with fries, and a chocolate shake."

"I don't think you should drown your sorrows, Maria," Liz said.

"I'm not drowning anything," Maria said. "I'm dressed up with no place to go."

"I'll take you to see the Hanging Toenails," said the guy in the suit. "My business is done for the day."

Maria looked at him archly. "Thanks, but I'm in a relationship."

"You just said you weren't," said the suit guy. "And even if you are, he just stood you up."

Maria shook her head. "Men," she said to Liz.

Liz put the order on the wheel. "I suppose you want me to make your shake."

"I just did my nails."

Liz sighed. Maria went behind the counter, poured herself some water, and took it to Alex's table.

"What's with you tonight?"

"Huh?" Alex was slurping the last bit of melted ice cream out of the bottom of his glass.

"You seem—I don't know—surly."

"Me?" Alex pushed the shake glass aside. "You're the one who won't call Michael."

Maria put an elbow on the table, then rested her chin in her hand. "You know, things are a lot easier if you talk about them."

"Yeah, you've proven that," said the guy in the suit. Liz glared at him, then reached into her pocket, took out his bill and slapped it beside his plate.

"There's nothing to talk about," Alex said.

"What about Isabel?"

"What about her?"

"Aren't you waiting for her?"

"No," Alex said, "and if I were, and if she was late, I would call her. It's just polite."

"All right." Maria reached into her purse and pulled out her cell phone. She dialed Michael's number with her right thumb, put the phone to her ear, and listened to it ring.

Alex, Liz, and the guy in the suit watched. The rings were so loud, Maria supposed that all three people could hear them. She let the phone ring fifteen times before hanging up.

No one spoke for a moment.

"Maybe he's on his way here," Liz finally said.

"Maybe," Maria said, but she didn't believe it.

"We need to get him a proper answering machine," Alex said.

"Yeah." Maria made herself smile.

"See?" the guy in the suit said. "Now, don't you feel better?"

"No," she said.

"Now you can go to the concert with me," the guy said. "You know what's going on."

But she didn't. Or she didn't want to believe that she did. Because if Michael wasn't here in fifteen minutes, she would know that he had stood her up. Or worse, that he had forgotten about her.

Maybe he was just trying to show her, yet again, that she needed to take some distance from him. He was so worried about that alien/human thing, about his "destiny" and all the danger he was putting her in.

Of course. That was what he was doing. He'd gotten

cold feet all over again, forgetting how strong she could be, how much she'd helped him in the past.

"So," the guy in the suit said as he got off the counter stool. "You want to go?"

Maria shook her head. "I just ordered."

"They haven't started it yet. You can cancel."

She gave him her prettiest smile. "I'll wait for Michael. But you go. Maybe you'll meet someone there who's more your type."

"All right," he said, as he laid a twenty on the counter. "But I'd never stand you up."

"Sure you would," Maria said, as the suit let himself out the front door. "You men are all alike."

"Hey," Alex said. "That's not fair."

"Except for you, Alex." Maria patted his cheek. "You're the original nice guy."

"So that's what I'm doing wrong," he said. "I always knew it was something."

"You know, we could close early," Liz said, "and I'll help you look for Michael."

"How pathetic is that?" Maria shook her head. "Nope. You're stuck, Parker. I want a shake and that burger. Then you can take off your apron and join us. We'll have a good long talk. We haven't done that for a while—human to human."

"Might be nice to talk about something besides saving the world," Liz said.

"Yeah, life has gotten so darn serious," Alex said with a grin.

"I'd like to go through one week without some kind of alien-caused crisis," Maria said. "Do you think we can make a pact to stay out of trouble just until next Thursday?"

"I don't see why not," Liz said, as she scooped out ice cream for the third time that hour.

"Good," Alex said.

"That means my only chore for the rest of the week is killing Michael." Maria grinned. "And I'm going to enjoy that."

3

March 24—Florence Junction, Arizona

The sound of a truck door slamming brought Jerry Daniels up out of his sound sleep on the old couch. The computer screen had switched to an old *Star Wars* screen saver and the room had gotten hot. Sun beat in through the living room's main window. Jerry reached under the couch and put his hand on the revolver there, ready for whoever would come through the door. It had sounded like Dane's truck door, but Jerry could never be too careful, considering what they were doing these days.

And this far out in the desert, he wasn't likely to be getting visitors. They were an hour south and east of Phoenix, and the house they were renting from an old rancher was down a long dirt driveway, tucked under some scraggy trees and against a rock bluff. Neither the driveway nor the house was visible from the two-lane road that left the small town of Florence Junction.

A moment later, Dane's whistling filtered through the

front door. Only Dane's warbling whistle could make Clint Black sound like opera. His boots pounded on the wooden porch steps, and Jerry relaxed.

Dane Hansen never seemed to be able to walk twenty feet without whistling. Considering that he wasn't that happy a person, the habit had always seemed odd to Jerry.

Jerry let go of the revolver and swung his legs off the couch. No need to let Dane know just how nervous he'd been. Dane might worry about keeping the gun around and that would be bad for both of them. Jerry was the brains, but Dane was the worrier, and sometimes he took matters into his own hands.

Jerry would do everything he could to prevent that.

The front door burst open and Dane strode through, his mouth puckered in his whistle. Dane was still a young guy—in his late twenties—but he was big, and his size made him seem more mature than he was. At six-five and three hundred pounds, Dane dwarfed most people he met.

There hadn't been many men willing to go up against Dane in prison, and considering that all Dane had done in the joint was lift weights and work on getting bigger and stronger, not many would try him now, either.

Jerry and Dane had been on the same cell block at the Arizona State Penitentiary. Dane had taken a liking to Jerry's fast mouth and smart ideas. Dane's conversation left a lot to be desired, and he didn't bathe as often as he should, but Jerry befriended him all the same. Jerry was skinny and five-eight on a good day. He'd needed protection from the day he entered the joint and Dane had provided it.

No one messed with Dane's friends. Even now.

As weird luck would have it they had gotten out at the same time, two days before Christmas. When Jerry stumbled into the best money-making deal ever imagined, he called Dane to help him.

"You take care of the package?" Jerry asked, climbing from the couch and heading for the computer on the dining room table.

"Wrapped up and stored tighter than maximum security." Dane smiled. He had a tooth missing on the left side of his mouth and the smile had always seemed comical to Jerry. But men had been hurt for less than laughing at Dane's smile. "And look at this."

Dane tossed three small packages on the table beside the computer. All three were addressed to the same Scottsdale post office box.

Jerry picked up one package. It was heavier than he expected. He hefted it, weighing it with his hands. In the old days, before he got busted, he could tell a gram from half a gram without using a scale. The skill hadn't left him, but he wasn't dealing with powder any longer.

He ripped open the brown paper. Cash, just like he thought. And a lot of it. But the problem was that ten one hundred dollar bills felt the same as ten one dollar bills.

He flipped through the cash, happy to see that all were hundreds. Fifteen thousand. Just like the doctor ordered.

No wonder Dane was whistling.

Jerry chuckled. "Looks like we're gonna have to make up more serum."

"You sure there ain't newspaper in those bundles?" Dane asked, always the worrier.

Jerry would have been positive even without checking.

No parent buying serum for his child ever shorted the manufacturer. Not with a child's life at stake.

Still, Jerry thumbed through the cash a second time. "Positive," he said. Then he opened the other packages. Fifteen thousand in each of them.

Damn, this scheme was good. They were getting rich fast—and if they were careful, they'd have a big nest egg by the beginning of May.

"Well," Dane said, "if they sent real money, then we got more serum in the kitchen."

Jerry laughed, ripped the three names off the three packets, and tossed the money back to Dane to put in the "safe," a loose wall board in the hallway across from the bathroom. They had over two hundred thousand in there now. Jerry had figured they would double that and then split up and get out of the desert. At this rate, it wasn't going to take long.

Dane ruffled the money, double-checking Jerry, then turned and headed toward the hallway.

Jerry dropped into the old dining room chair and clicked off the screen saver. A moment later he was in the file with the names of the "clients." He clicked off the three who had paid today.

Then he logged on, using a stolen dormant account based in San Francisco, and checked his e-mail. Some woman wrote about her daughter, how ill the kid was and how much she needed this "cure" to save her. The other e-mail was from another parent whose name, so far, was only a numbered account, and the letter told yet another sob story.

Jerry was cautious about the second e-mail. He would

back-trace the account's owner in a minute. He wasn't going to get nailed by some fed pretending to be someone he wasn't.

The third e-mail was from a desperate couple whose kid was on his last legs. They'd run out of options and they were running out of time. Jerry smiled. These were the kind of people he liked the best.

He sent each a standard reply letter about how sorry he was, how he wasn't sure his serum would be right for their child. Later tonight, through other connections, he'd get information about all of the new clients, to make sure it wasn't the police. It hadn't been so far, and he doubted it would ever be. The clients who contacted him were desperate people looking for help for their children.

Without fail each client would answer his I'm-not-sure letter with a begging, please-give-my-child-a-chance letter. The scam always worked.

His cover was so simple. He claimed to be a research doctor, working underground on a serum the drug companies wanted off the market because it was too effective for most childhood diseases. He had gotten the idea after the so-called miracle in the children's ward in the hospital in Phoenix. Since no one else was claiming credit, he figured he would.

It was so easy. No one knew why the kids healed. Everyone had a different story. The kids made it even easier. They had seen an angel—a guy—who had told them to go back to sleep. That was it.

Jerry claimed he put the serum in their IV tubes and the kids had recovered within a short period of time. A few of the kids had seen him, he said, and called him an angel. The other kids "remembered" that they had seen him, too.

It was that simple.

People believed what they wanted to believe. And desperate people made the best believers of all.

Jerry told this story on a few web sites, and added a bunch of hooey about how the FDA had withdrawn approval of his miracle serum after protest from the drug companies. The drug companies protested, Jerry said, because he had refused to sell them the patent and they would lose millions of dollars on their other drugs if his was ever approved.

Because these parents had already been hurt by the medical system, because they had been grasping at straws and having those straws denied them, because they had already fought with their insurance companies over experimental treatments, they were easy marks. They believed him.

The more they wanted a miracle, the more they believed that the FDA worked with the drug companies, that corporate medicine was just in it for the money, that one single research scientist held the key to a cure.

Years ago, when he started working cons, he'd met up with a guy who pulled off big deals. At that time, Jerry was doing penny-ante stuff, confusing a mark and having that person empty her bank account to help a "homeless" man, or scamming credit card numbers in a made-up fund-raising campaign.

But the guy he met was raising thousands every day on a real estate scam so outrageous Jerry wondered how anyone would believe it. So he finally asked the guy.

The guy had smiled. "The bigger the lie, the easier it is," he had said.

"What do you mean?" Jerry had asked.

"People question little lies," the guy had said, "but they swallow the big ones like a piece of chocolate cake. I guess lies are easier to take in one big chunk. Try it next time. You'll see what I mean."

So Jerry had tried it. He told people that a landmark building in St. Paul was going to slide into the Mississippi. He dummied up a few newspaper clippings about it, made a presentation, and walked away with a cool twenty grand.

His mistake—and the reason he got sent up—was because he wasn't comfortable with the big lie. He went back to his penny-ante stuff, believing he couldn't come up with something big in every community he visited.

He got caught on the very first scam, and vowed never to do small stuff again. While he was in jail, he got permission to use the prison's computer equipment, taking classes, improving, and becoming a model prisoner.

By the time he got out of the joint, he was ready to pull the biggest lie of all and use the most modern of tools— the Internet.

The so-called miracle in Phoenix provided his big lie. He just played into it. And he'd been doing it for three months, so if anyone else did come forward, it would be hard for them to take credit.

The clients bought right into his selfless act. He claimed he hadn't been able to bear seeing children die on Christmas Eve, which was why he had gone into the children's ward in Phoenix and given them all his serum.

Plus he was being smart, to keep the police away as

long as possible. He didn't claim his serum worked on every child. He used the word "experimental" a lot on his web site and in his first e-mail response, he reminded the parents that results would vary.

He only asked for a $15,000 "gift" to help him cover his research costs. He didn't demand it, telling the families to pay whatever they could afford. Never had anyone come up with less than the asked-for $15,000, and twice people had sent along extra money.

Also, to keep this going as long as possible, Jerry did send the clients a serum, using Dane as a delivery man, meeting the clients, and making a big deal out of how to handle the serum. Dane had even come up with the idea of putting each treatment into a small bottle, with a cork, packed in a cheap ice chest—perfect props that cost them almost nothing.

The serum was made up of a combination of different cough medicines found in any drugstore. If nothing else, the children didn't cough much after taking his stuff. And he gave each client just enough for one full treatment, a single dose, making sure the kid took it all, including drinking the water rinsed from the bottle, so there would be almost nothing left to analyze.

Jerry had had unhappy clients, sure, since his serum did nothing. But with each one he acted like the upset doctor through his e-mail contacts, trying to get them to understand that his serum didn't work for everyone yet. He would ask for all the details about the child's condition, and then tell the upset client that as soon as the next level serum was finished, which would be any day, he would send along another treatment, free, and in the meantime, they should just keep their children in the hospital and under normal treatment procedures. So far that promise of a free second chance had kept anyone from running to the police.

"Two hundred and thirty-five big ones in there," Dane said, shaking his head as he came from the hallway. "I got to hand it to you, Jerry, this is a sweet deal."

"Fifteen clients paid, two, maybe three more today," Jerry said, looking up from the computer. "Another eight to ten sick kids and we'll be out of here."

Dane laughed. "I can hardly wait."

Then, whistling a Travis Tritt song, he headed for the kitchen to make up the phoney serum as Jerry went back to work on the computer, spreading the word, searching for that next desperate parent, the one who would lead him to the next and the next, until he and Dane were rich men.

Rich and free men. Men who would never, ever get caught.

4

March 24—Unknown location

Michael's head hurt. The pain was so great that the back of his skull throbbed. He knew, if he opened his eyes, that light would stab them, making the pain worse.

He tried to reach his head, then realized that his arms were trapped. He rolled on his stomach, his body making a thump against a wood floor.

He'd been attacked in front of the apartment building. He should have been on grass or on concrete. His stomach turned, nausea filling him. There was a strange smell in his nostrils, a dry medicinal odor that clung to everything.

His hands were tied. He could feel the rope cutting into his skin.

He still didn't want to open his eyes. Let the nausea pass. Let the dizziness, the pain, move past him.

Something was very wrong.

Beneath the medicinal smell, he caught a whiff of exhaust. The smell was coming from his clothing, almost as if he'd been standing near a running car.

But he hadn't been. He'd been trying to see Maria.

Maria! His eyes fluttered, started to open, and he moaned. He was really late now. She'd never forgive him. She probably had no idea where he was.

Neither did Max.

Neither did he.

He remembered the movement of a car, the sickly, sliding out of control feeling that he used to have when he was trying to sleep in the back of his dad's pickup. His dad never bothered to buckle him in, or let him sit on the seat beside him. At night, if Michael was along, he'd fall asleep in the back near the wheels and the cans of paint and the tire chains.

Sometimes they'd even slid into him as the truck went around a curve.

Something slid into him not too long ago. He remembered it gouging into his thigh, the pain pulling him out of his groggy sleep.

His eyelids felt stuck together. He blinked again, then peered through his eyelashes. Walls, floor. Light coming from a bulb overhead, blinding him.

"Not yet," a man's voice said.

A cloth covered Michael's mouth and nose. A hand pressed the cloth into his face. He struggled, the nausea growing worse. The medicinal smell was back, dry, antiseptic, taking the air from his lungs.

He kicked, but his feet were bound, too. He tried to roll away, but another hand held him. He had to focus. If he could focus, he could use his powers, blast this guy off him—

But his ability to think was evaporating. He was losing consciousness again. He fought to stay awake, but he could sense himself spiraling away, becoming nothing.

Going nowhere.

Unable to save himself.

March 24—Roswell, New Mexico

"This is wrong," Liz said.

Maria's fingers felt along the top of the doorframe. Lots of dust, most of it trickling down into her hair and her eyes. Good thing she wasn't dressed up this morning. She probably looked like a wreck already.

She balanced precariously on the empty cardboard boxes one of Michael's neighbors had left in the hallway.

"Maria," Liz said. "We shouldn't be doing this."

Maria stretched to her full length, reaching for the far corner. "What do you suggest we do, Liz?"

"I don't know." Liz looked over her shoulder. "Maybe Michael just went somewhere, you know?"

"If he went off somewhere, he would have told me."

"He hasn't in the past."

Maria lost her balance, tottered, then jumped off the boxes. "Well, that was the past."

Her hands were covered with grime. Obviously, nothing had been on top of that doorframe for a long time.

"What's with Michael?" she asked. "Most people hide a key somewhere in case they lock themselves out."

Liz raised her eyebrows. "Is that what you were looking for? A key?"

"What did you think I was doing? Searching for a secret unlocking mechanism?"

"How should I know? You're being weird."

"You're being weird. There has to be a key somewhere."

"No, there doesn't," Liz said.

Maria frowned at her.

"It's *Michael*," Liz said.

Maria let out a small sigh and then shook her head. What was she thinking? Michael could change matter with his bare hands. What did he need a key for? If he locked himself out, he could probably make the lock turn just by putting his palm against the doorknob.

She leaned against the wall and slid down. "I'm so worried."

"I know," Liz said.

"He didn't answer the phone all night."

"You called him all night?"

Maria glared at her. "It was your idea."

"Actually, it was Alex's."

"Whatever. I called, and there's been no answer."

"Do you think he's hurt?"

"He will be if he's just not answering the phone," Maria said.

"And the door," Liz said. "I don't know how anyone could have survived all that pounding."

Maria's hand wasn't surviving that well, either. She'd used the side of her fist and now it was hot and achy. One of the neighbors had even peered out, just to see what she was doing.

No Good Deed

"Trying to wake him up," Maria had said, and some-how the neighbor had understood. Maria didn't want to know why the neighbor knew about Michael's sleeping habits.

"Maybe we should get Max," Liz said.

"That's your solution for everything, isn't it?" Maria asked. " 'Let's get Max.' Well, we'll feel pretty dumb if Michael's sleeping on the couch with his headphones on like he was on Valentine's Day."

"I think that was on purpose," Liz mumbled.

"I heard that," Maria said.

Liz shrugged, then extended her hand. Maria took it, and let Liz help her to her feet.

"Either we try to go in or we give up or we get Max," Liz said.

Maria reached into her purse and took out her wallet.

"What are you doing?" Liz asked.

Maria pulled out her MasterCard and waved it in front of Liz's face. "Trying to get in."

Liz crossed her arms. "That only works in the movies."

"No, it doesn't." Maria faced Michael's door, blocking the neighbor's view of what she was doing with her body. She slid the credit card along the doorframe and heard a satisfying click. Then she shoved the door open.

"You've done this before," Liz said with awe.

Maria smiled. "Only on this door. It has a flimsy lock."

She stepped inside. Sunlight filtered through the blinds on the windows. The place smelled faintly of ham-burger grease—Michael's diet was remarkably similar at home and at work—and of Michael's hair gel.

A pair of battered tennis shoes lay on the living room

41

floor, complete with crumpled socks. The couch looked rumpled, and the remote was on the arm, where Michael kept it when he'd been watching a lot of TV.

Maria touched the television set. It was cool.

Liz hovered near the door, glancing into the hallway.

"Close the door, will you?" Maria asked. "No sense letting the entire neighborhood know we're here."

Liz closed the door and leaned on it. "I don't like breaking in."

"Michael won't know."

"Unless he's here."

But Maria could already tell he wasn't here. She was very attuned to everything about Michael, his movements, his voice, the way he turned his head. Even the feeling in a room changed when he entered it.

He hadn't been here for some time.

Still, she inspected all the rooms, from the bathroom with its shaving equipment on the sink and the towels crumpled on the floor. She touched one of the towels. It was dry, and she could tell from the position it was in that Michael had left it on the floor wet.

Then she glanced into the bedroom. The bed was unmade, and it was impossible to tell if Michael had slept in it last night or not. His shirts were hung neatly in the closet, and his jeans were draped over a chair.

His jacket and his car keys were gone, though.

Maria frowned. "Hey, Liz. Do you see Michael's keys?"

"No." Liz's voice filtered in from the living room. It sounded like she hadn't moved at all from the front door.

"Would you check, please?"

Liz's sigh echoed all the way from the living room, but

Maria could hear her rustling around. Maria checked the bedroom dresser and the scarred nightstand, finding nothing. She didn't look in the drawers, though. She didn't want to be perceived as that much of a snoop.

When she went into the kitchen, she saw Liz gingerly lifting the lids of old pizza boxes and looking beneath them.

'No keys, right?" Maria said.

Liz nodded.

"Michael's car's outside."

"So?" Liz said. "The apartment was locked."

Maria frowned. "Yeah, but usually if Michael walks anywhere, he doesn't go far. Otherwise he drives."

Liz nodded. She knew that. "Maybe he walked some-where."

"When?" Maria asked. "He didn't answer the phone this morning."

"How many times did you call?"

"Enough to give you some statistics," Maria said. "I don't like this."

"Me either." It sounded like an admission from Liz. "What do you think we should do?"

Maria looked around the messy, but familiar apart-ment. It seemed very empty without Michael inside. "I hate to tell you this, girl, but I think we should call Max."

Liz winced and looked away. Her relationship with Max had been difficult all year. She kept expecting him to run off with Tess. Liz had broken it off with him, but she still cared for him, so much that it hurt her to talk about him.

Maria would have known that without Liz saying a word to her, but Liz did confide in her. Liz had to confide in someone.

"You want me to call him?" Maria asked.

"No," Liz said, pulling her cell phone out of her purse. "I'll do it."

An hour later, the old gang met at the Crashdown. It felt like it used to feel—back in the days after Liz got shot and Michael saved her, when Liz, Maria, and Alex were just learning that their friends were aliens. Or it would have felt that way if Michael were around.

Maria had taken over a booth in the back of the restaurant. She sat on the side facing the door, so she could see anyone who came in or out. Her cell phone's ringer was placed on high, just in case Michael called.

Ever since she left his apartment, her stomach had been tied into knots.

Max sat next to her. Isabel and Alex sat across from her. They'd all ordered Cokes, and the Evanses had ordered breakfast. Alex had stolen a piece of toast from Isabel's plate before she coated her food in Tabasco sauce, and unlike times in the past, Isabel didn't seem to mind.

Liz had her uniform on, since she had to work the lunch shift. But she hadn't punched in yet. She wasn't due to start for another half hour.

It had been Max's idea to meet her, and a good thing too, because Maria had a hunch Liz had forgotten that she was supposed to work.

"We should probably approach this like real detectives." Alex took a bite from the piece of toast. "You know, figure out who saw him last and all that."

Max had been the one who was most upset by the fact that Michael's keys were gone and his car was there. He had confirmed Maria's suspicions—that something was wrong with all of this. Even Isabel had mentioned that Michael had planned to come to the Crashdown the night before.

"Well," Max said, "I watched part of the game with him, but I had to get home to dinner."

"Even though you'd already had pizza," Isabel said, stirring her red-coated eggs, but not eating them.

Max shrugged. "You can't watch basketball without pizza."

Isabel shook her head.

"Where was he going to go after the game?" Maria asked.

"He said he was coming here," Max said. "I reminded him that he had to leave before eight no matter what was happening on the screen. He said he knew that."

Maria could just imagine how he had said it, too, with that surly resentful tone he used whenever he was told to do something he had already planned to do.

"I saw him yesterday afternoon," Isabel said, "and he asked me…"

Her voice trailed off and she glanced at Alex. He was leaning away from her, as if he didn't want to be that close.

"Asked you what?" Maria asked.

"Nothing important," Isabel said, lying poorly as she usually did.

"Asked you *what*?" Maria asked again.

Isabel's lips thinned and she stirred her eggs some more. "If you were going to get dressed up or not, and if he was expected to do some date thing or if he could just show up and have a good time."

Maria felt a flash of irritation mixed with a bit of amusement. That sounded like Michael.

"What did you tell him?" she asked.

"That I didn't know." Isabel looked at her. "And I didn't. You mentioned the Hanging Toenails to me, but you never said whether or not you planned a date."

"She planned a date," Alex said dryly.

"But Michael didn't know that, right?" Liz asked. Because they all knew that if Michael had known it, he might have found some way out of it.

"He was still planning to come and see you when I left at six," Max said to Maria.

Michael had been there at six. And by nine, he didn't answer his phone. Her stomach turned and she had to look away from the Tabasco-covered eggs on the table.

She wasn't sure what she wanted anymore, for Michael to be off on some fool's errand, or for him to have forgotten her and forgotten to talk with Max. Because all the other choices weren't any good at all.

The door to the Crashdown opened. Maria squinted at it, trying to see past the bright sunlight, which was having the effect of blinding her.

Then the door closed, and she saw Tess and Kyle hurrying toward the table.

Liz was convinced that Tess wanted Max again—that theirs was probably a true love that survived over the ages, and it would only take time for them to realize it. All the while, of course, hoping that she was really Max's true love, as he had told her nearly two years before.

Maria wrapped her hand around her cold Coke glass. Liz stiffened as she watched Tess approach.

"You found him yet?" Tess asked Max, and Maria blinked in surprise. She hadn't realized that anyone had told Tess that Michael was missing.

"No," Max said.

"Where have you looked?"

"Just his usual haunts."

Liz was twisting her fingers together. Maria wanted to reach across Max and make Liz stop. It was irritating, and it wasn't hiding how she felt at all.

"What about the woods?" Kyle asked.

"We haven't looked there yet," Isabel said.

None of them were fond of the woods anymore, not after the whole incident with the alien crystals that could have destroyed everything.

Tess grabbed a chair from a nearby table. She sat on it, then leaned forward. "What about the granilith?"

She spoke so softly that Maria could barely hear her. Tess had meant the question for Max and Max alone.

"He has no reason to go there," Max said.

"You don't know that."

Max winced. He and Michael weren't as close as they used to be and everyone knew it.

"Do you think someone might have forced him to go there?" Isabel asked.

"If they did, they'd have to be really strong," Maria said. She spoke louder than she had intended to. Everyone looked at her. She shrugged. "It would be hard to make Michael do anything he didn't want to do, even if he didn't have powers."

"That's true," Max said. "But Tess is right. We're not done searching. We're going to have to split up and see what we can find."

He glanced at Liz, who shoved her hands into the pockets of her uniform.

"I guess I'll stay here and work, in case he shows up," Liz said.

Max nodded. "I think that's a good idea. If you get a chance, keep calling the apartment. Maybe he'll come back and not even know that we're looking for him."

Maria slid her Coke back and forth across the table. Michael would be protesting right now. He hated it when Max gave orders. Yet it felt right. Max did have natural leadership skills.

"Alex and Kyle, why don't you check the woods?"

"Great," Alex said. "We get all the fun jobs."

"I don't think they should go there alone," Isabel said, looking at Max.

"You mean without protection?" Kyle asked, his tone dry. "Us poor little ol' powerless humans?"

Tess elbowed him. "She's right. There's—"

"Beasties in them thar woods," Alex said with a smile. "I, for one, don't mind a bodyguard."

I just bet you don't, Maria almost said, but caught herself before the words escaped.

"All right," Max said. "Isabel, you go with them."

Isabel leaned back, looking satisfied. She shot a small glance at Alex, of the kind that Alex used to give her. What was going on with the two of them?

Maria had no idea and at the moment, she wasn't sure she cared.

"Tess and I," Max said, lowering his voice to a whisper, "will look at the granilith."

Liz bowed her head. Maria almost protested, but stopped herself. Ever since they'd discovered the granilith, the four aliens had been protective of it. Maria sometimes got the sense they were afraid of it—maybe because they didn't know all that it could do.

"We'll meet back here in a few hours," Max said.

"I think we should call my dad," Kyle said.

Everyone looked at him.

"It hasn't come to that yet, has it?" Isabel asked.

"Come to what? He's not sheriff anymore." Kyle said that last with a touch of bitterness. "But he's good in situations like this."

"That's true," Liz said. "And he'll know how important it is to find Michael and why."

Her words hung over them for a moment. It wasn't like some high school boy had disappeared on his girlfriend. Michael's mysterious disappearance could mean anything from a Skin attack to problems with the FBI to something as innocent as getting lost in the woods.

Maria swallowed. "You forgot me," she said to Max.

"No, he didn't," Liz said. "He probably figures you'd stay here with me."

Max's dark eyes met Maria's. He had expected her to stay here, sipping soda and going quietly crazy. Well, she wasn't the kind of person to do that.

But she didn't want to go to the woods and she didn't want to tag along with the former Mr. and Mrs. Max on their trip to the granilith.

"I'll go see Brody," Maria said. "Maybe he's been abducted again."

"You'd think we would have heard," Max said.

"Maybe," Isabel said. "But maybe not. We're not privy to everything they do, Max."

Max nodded. "He might be able to use some of that equipment to help us, too. Maybe he has some ideas."

"That's what I figured," Maria said.

Everyone was looking at her, as if she were about to break or something. She had no idea why they expected that. Michael was missing, yes, but he'd gone off and done things on his own before. This incident might be just like those were—infuriating, but ultimately innocent.

"Well," she said, "what are we waiting for?"

And with that, the entire group was moving. Tess slid her chair back, Alex and Isabel were getting out of the booth, Liz was heading toward the back.

Only Max hadn't moved, effectively blocking Maria in the booth.

"What else do you know?" he asked softly.

"Nothing," she said.

He sighed.

"You're worried, aren't you?" she asked.

He nodded.

"This time it feels different, doesn't it?" she asked.

"Yeah, and I don't know why."

Because Michael had settled down. He'd made some hard choices this year, and he knew that his friends cared about him. He had told Maria more than once he wasn't going to screw any of that up.

"We'll find him, Max," she said with a conviction she didn't feel.

"I hope so," Max said.

"He can take care of himself." Maria had been repeating that to herself over and over. It felt strange to say it to Max.

"He's been able to so far," Max said. "But someday we're going to face the things that made us leave our planet—and I'm not sure we're up to that."

"You think that's what's happened to Michael?"

"I don't know," Max said. "But you know me. I always expect the worst."

He slid out of the booth. Maria watched him go, her hands shaking. He expected the worst, and so did she.

And this time, their worst was something she didn't want to think about—ever.

5

Katie no longer looked like she belonged in her bedroom.

Chad Newcomb closed the curtains of the window closest to the bed so that the sunlight wouldn't fall across Katie's eyes. He kept the other windows open, though, so that she could see the desert garden they'd planted together the summer before.

Not that it mattered. The morning had left her exhausted. It had left him exhausted as well, but he had strength to spare.

She didn't.

She looked so small and frail in her bed, the pink frills that he and Maggie had picked out for her nearly enveloping her. Chad sat on the side of the bed, sinking into the thick mattress.

His body ached with exhaustion. He'd pulled a muscle in his back just that morning and it spasmed now, making him wince.

He brushed a strand of hair off Katie's face. She didn't even move. Her skin was hot to the touch, and her eyes were so recessed into her face that she almost didn't look human anymore.

Maybe he shouldn't have brought her home, after all. As the doctor had said, caring for her was a full-time job. More than full-time. It took vigilance every hour out of twenty-four.

And Chad had to do it alone.

He wiped his clammy hands on his knees. He wished Maggie were here. She would be able to tell him what to do. He wished someone could.

The doctor had tried, but that man had lost his credibility with Chad a month ago. They'd thought Katie had a new viral disease, a mutant strain of some deadly childhood illness. The aggressive treatment had made her worse.

So then they figured it was an obscure form of leukemia, but the leukemia never showed up in her blood tests. In fact, all that showed up in her blood tests were elevated levels of white blood cells—which would be what happened whenever the body fought an infection.

Then the doctor said that she might have caught a strain of a difficult-to-kill virus that lurked in hospitals, made stronger because of the all the antibacterial agents used in hospitals as well as the antibiotics. He'd proclaimed antibiotics useless against Katie's disease, and took her off her regimen.

She'd nearly died that night.

From that moment on, Chad had sought second and third opinions, all of them expressing bafflement. One doctor wanted to fly Katie to the world-famous Mayo

Clinic. Another wanted to check her heart. Still a third believed that she was suffering from some lifelong vitamin deficiency, which led to her incredible thinness.

Chad could explain the thinness. Katie hadn't eaten properly since Thanksgiving. Her body wasn't taking in any nutrition despite the IVs that the hospital kept attached to her arm—part of the time, anyway. The rest of the time, they forced her to eat regular food, apparently afraid she'd become unable to.

She had been on the food part of the cycle this week. That was one of the reasons he felt all right about removing her from the hospital. They weren't doing anything there that he couldn't do at home.

He kept thinking back to that Christmas Miracle, finding his mind going over and over the if-onlys.

He had told the doctor that he wanted Katie to die at home. The doctor had said that Katie would die at home if Chad took her away.

But Chad knew better. He had brought article after article he'd downloaded from the Internet to the hospital, asking the doctor to try new things, and the doctor had refused. So had the second- and third-opinion doctors, and all the others he had called.

Some of them had used the phrase "false hope," while others had used the word "scam." And they used those terms no matter what he brought to them. It seemed that they found any form of experimentation, of alternative medicine, illegitimate and not worthy of their time.

But it wasn't their time that was being lost. It was Katie's.

She was dying, and somehow Chad had to stop it.

He brushed his hand over her hot little face one more time, and stood. The movement was difficult. The sore muscles in his legs had gotten stiff in the short time he'd been sitting. He had no idea how he had let himself get so out of shape. Apparently four months without exercise was taking its toll.

He glanced at the IV leaning against the wall. He had it if he needed it, along with the nutrient bags. It was amazing how much medical paraphernalia a person could buy on the Internet. He'd even found pharmacies that would sell him medication without double-checking the signatures on the prescriptions he'd faxed.

He got enough stuff to keep Katie going here for a little while at least.

Reaching to the nightstand, he grabbed the baby monitor that he and Maggie had bought when Maggie was pregnant with Katie, and turned it on. Then he left the room, picking the other monitor off the hallway table where he'd left it. He made sure he turned that monitor on as well.

He'd told Katie he was going to do this, that this was how she could find him, no matter where he was.

Not that he ever planned to leave her side for long.

He went into the dining room and hit the space bar on his computer. The screen saver—a drawing Katie had made the year before—disappeared and his e-mail program popped up. He had left it open to the letter he'd received that morning, before he'd gotten Katie from the hospital.

Chad stared at the letter again, feeling the same confusion he'd felt when he opened the letter. Confusion and strength at the same time. He finally had two chances to save his daughter.

Two, not one.

The letter was from a researcher who claimed he had a serum that would cure most childhood diseases. The researcher said he'd been the man behind the Christmas Miracle at the hospital. He'd used his serum there, even though it hadn't been approved by the FDA, because he'd known it would work.

He wanted to get the word out because the drug companies and the hospitals were preventing anyone from using this cure.

Chad remembered finding information on this man, feeling that the researcher was irresponsible (what if the stuff hadn't worked?) and a hero (because the stuff had worked) all at the same time.

He double-checked the guy's credentials on the Internet, made sure the man was legit, and then he'd sent the money. Fifteen thousand was a lot of cash, no matter how rich a man was. It made him uncomfortable to send that much money through the mails, but he could afford to lose it.

Even if he couldn't afford to lose it, he would have sent it. After all, Katie's life was priceless—if he had to spend fifteen million to save her, he'd find the cash somehow.

He would do anything for her.

But that had been days ago, and he hadn't heard. He logged on two and three times an hour, hoping to hear something. But as the days went by, he became convinced he was the victim of a scam.

After he'd already given up and moved on to a new plan, he got this morning's e-mail.

It was a letter from the researcher. He had gotten Chad's money and wanted to deliver the serum. It was, apparently, illegal to send unapproved drugs through the mail, and the researcher didn't want to put Chad in jeopardy from the law—not a man with a sick child.

The researcher probably didn't want to put himself in jeopardy either, but Chad still appreciated the restraint. He printed out the letter with its instructions to the delivery site, and stared at them for a moment.

The e-mail had been sent this morning.

He logged on, sent an e-mail saying he'd be at the delivery site, and logged off. He had no idea how he'd go there with Katie so ill, but he'd find a way.

There was always a way.

The phone rang.

Chad started. The ringer sounded loud, even though he had it turned down so that it wouldn't disturb Katie. He sat very still as the ringing continued, until his answering machine in the kitchen picked up.

He heard his own voice, mixing with Katie's, a six-month-old tape he sometimes replayed when he was really feeling hopeless, just so that he could hear her fluted giggle at the tape's end. Then their voices ended, followed by the digital beep, and a familiar male voice spoke softly into the machine.

Chad only caught a few words, but he didn't have to listen. He knew what the message would be. He'd already gotten two others just like it on the machine.

It was Katie's doctor, begging Chad to bring her back to the hospital. The doctor was afraid she'd die without continued treatment.

So was Chad. But the treatment the doctor had been giving her wasn't consistent, and it was time for Chad to try new things.

Maybe this weekend would mark the point at which Katie would finally turn around, finally get better.

He had two chances now. And that was two chances more than he'd had yesterday.

The machine clicked off, and Chad stood. He grabbed the baby monitor, holding it to his ear for a moment. Katie's breathing sounded even and regular, just like it used to when she was in her crib. He knew that was a lie—her breathing might have been even, but nothing about her was regular anymore.

Sometimes he sat up in the house late at night, listening to its creaks and ticks, realizing that Katie might be stuck forever as a child, never to go to high school, kiss a boy, get married or have children of her own. She would never get the chance to succeed at a career or yell at her father or have an intellectual debate.

She'd never have a chance to grow old.

He couldn't allow that. Maggie hadn't had a chance to grow old. The last thing he wanted—the last thing Maggie would have wanted—was for the same thing to happen to their child.

Chad was shaking. He'd never flown solo like this before. He was doing things he would have thought crazy two years ago. Sending cash through the mail on a desperate hope. Taking a child out of the hospital against doctor's orders.

And then, everything he had done last night.

He walked down the hallway and peered into Katie's

room. She hadn't moved. The sunlight had, though. It was covering her legs, illuminating that bright pink bedspread, making it seem almost neon.

Chad smiled at her, even though he knew she couldn't see him, and then continued past her room to the guest bedroom.

The curtains were all drawn in this room, making it seem like twilight. Still, he could make out the form on the bed.

The young man he'd taken from Roswell last night. The boy, really, because up close he'd looked even younger than he had that night in the hospital.

It had been quite a struggle to get him here. Even though Chad was athletic, he wasn't used to carrying a tall teenager over his shoulder like a sack of potatoes. Nor was he used to putting that teenager into the trunk of his car.

His shaking grew worse as he thought about all he'd done, all the laws he'd broken.

For Katie. It was all for Katie.

And if she lived, it would all be worthwhile.

6

March 24th—Roswell, New Mexico

Nila Spence settled into her booth in the funkiest diner she'd ever been in, and that was saying something. The Crashdown had spaceburgers that were covered with little green goo. It served "out of this world" shakes, and the menu claimed it spoke the universal language of pie.

She wasn't going to try that. Her arteries had hardened the moment she breathed the air in this place. Unfortunately, the air smelled good. The burgers looked thick and charbroiled, and the fries crispy. Even the salads looked delicious—and artery-busting—piled high with meat and hard-boiled eggs and so much cheese that she had to search for the lettuce.

She hadn't ordered any of that, although she was tempted to have a shake—the Weather Balloon, with its silvery photograph, looked the most tempting. "A delicious mix of vanilla and blueberry ice creams, mixed with a secret ingredient, guaranteed to linger on the tongue—

and the memory—forever." Someone had had an attack of the cutes writing the menu—and had done a really good job.

Just like they'd done with the décor. She particularly liked the waitress uniforms: done in fifties' diner drab blue, covered with a silvery apron and silver headbands complete with bobbing antennae. The best part about the outfits was that the waitresses seemed comfortable in them. In Phoenix, she knew, waitresses always apologized for the way they looked, even when they were wearing more or less normal outfits.

She couldn't imagine how they'd feel in this getup.

Nila reached into her bag and pulled out her laptop, shoving aside two nearly empty bottles of Tabasco sauce, a full ketchup, salt and pepper shakers, and an old-fashioned napkin holder just to make room. She had to make notes about this place. She wasn't sure how she'd use it, but she knew she would. Local color was what made feature writing into an art.

And Roswell had a lot of local color.

She'd spent the morning looking at the goofy tourist shops, with their alien-heads-in-a-jar, glowing green alien dolls, and I'M FROM ANOTHER PLANET bumper stickers. Somehow she'd expected those places.

But she hadn't expected such seriousness in the UFO museum. She'd paid the small entry fee to wander through it, even though its proprietor, Brody, had made it clear that he couldn't see her until later in the day. She wanted to get a sense of the way this man spent his days.

She'd spoken to Davis on the phone before she'd made the almost seven-hour drive from Phoenix. His accent had surprised her—she hadn't expected him to be British. She had expected his politeness, but not his firmness when he turned down the interview.

"Mr. Davis," she had said. "It's your chance to tell your story."

"It's not my story," he had said. "It's Sydney's. And she's too young to be the focus of any kind of attention. I didn't let the local TV reporters talk to her, and I'm not letting you talk to her, either."

"Mr. Davis, what I'm doing here is deep background. I work for a legitimate newspaper. I don't use quotes unless I can verify the facts with two other sources. The experiences of a little girl, one who had, hours before, been quite ill, probably won't qualify."

"Pretty words," he had said, "but I won't trust my daughter's privacy to probably and maybes."

Nila had met with this kind of resistance many times in her career. "How about this? Let me send you some clippings so that you can see my work. You'll know I'm legitimate then. I'll also send you the name and number of the features editor, and some of the other editors I've worked for freelance. I don't do sensational stories, Mr. Davis."

"Then why are you doing this?" he'd asked, and she had smiled, knowing he was hooked.

"Because something or someone healed those children that night," she had said. "I want to find out who or what it was."

She didn't tell him about the doctor she had discovered on the Internet, the man who claimed to be behind the entire event. She had stumbled upon his site while doing an article on local scam artists, and its reasoned, calm approach to medicine had alarmed her.

People in desperate situations often believed in absurd things. Those people were the ones most likely to be taken in by scams like this one. She had finished her general article, then downloaded the web site's home page and taken it to her editor.

For her editor, it was the Phoenix connection that made the story relevant. The paper was already in trouble for not covering the Christmas Miracle—at least, not in any meaningful way. They had done a six-paragraph article on page fifteen of the Metro section, explaining that a ward full of children had gotten well on Christmas Eve—and those children attributed their recoveries to an "angel."

The local TV stations and the rival paper had played up the news big time. People wrote letters to her paper, complaining that the paper hadn't given it space, and the city desk editor had had to write an editorial defending his choice not to cover the story.

It was sensationalism of the worst sort, he had said. There were no facts to support a Christmas miracle. People got well all the time. Just because there had been a disturbance on the ward and the children felt better didn't mean it was time to start believing in Santa Claus, the Easter bunny, and angels who selectively healed a ward full of sick children.

That, of course, had been the worst thing he could have written, even if it was true. Journalism's pendulum had swung again—and things like facts were getting in the way of all the bunk people wanted to believe. The paper lost some subscribers over its handling of the

Christmas Miracle, and was looking for a way to get those subscribers back.

Nila had been aware of all of this peripherally, of course, but it hadn't been on her mind when she'd brought the print-out of the home page to her editor. However, it was on his. He wanted her to find out the secret to the Christmas Miracle, no matter how long it took. And he wanted a series of articles on what was clearly a scam, designed to bilk the sick and the despondent.

This was the kind of story she liked the best, one that would cure ills and expose wrong-doing. It was the reason she had become a journalist in the first place.

"Hi."

A husky voice brought her out of her reverie. One of the waitresses, a tired teenage girl with chocolate colored eyes, looked at her expectantly. She held a notepad in her slender hands.

"Are you ready to order?"

"Yeah," Nila said. "I take it you don't have any low-fat food?"

The girl laughed. "We did, but we took it off the menu. No one ever bought it. I guess when people come to a diner, they want burgers and fries."

True enough. Nila wasn't feeling like bucking the trend. "How's the Galaxy Burger?"

"Spicy with the pepperjack cheese," the waitress said. "But it's one of our most popular items."

The door opened behind her and she looked over her shoulder, her expression taut.

Nila frowned. The waitress, whose badge said her

name was Liz, seemed nervous, almost on edge, as if she expected something bad to happen.

"Is everything all right?" Nila asked.

"Yeah," Liz said, but there was no conviction in her voice. A couple walked into the restaurant and she relaxed slightly, as if they were not who she was expecting. "What do you want to drink?"

"Well, I've been toying with one of those shakes."

Liz smiled. It lit up her entire face and made her beautiful, despite her exhaustion. "They're good, but they're not low-fat."

"I don't care. When in Roswell, you know."

"No," Liz said, puzzled, "I don't."

Nila sighed. Kids weren't learning the right things anymore. "I was mangling an old quote. When in Rome, do what the Romans do, or something like that."

"Oh." Liz held her pen over her ticket book. "Did you want a shake then?"

"I guess so," Nila said. "How's the Weather Balloon?"

"A little gimmicky. Our double-chocolate is better."

"It would kill me," Nila said. "Let's go with old-fashioned vanilla, shall we?"

"All right." Liz pocketed her ticket book. "Is there anything else?"

"Yes," Nila said. "What is it that Roswellians do on a beautiful Saturday?"

Liz shrugged. "I'm always working."

And then she walked away.

Nila watched her go. Liz put up the order, but before she started the shake, she picked up the phone. Nila started to look away. After all, she'd been a teenage girl once, and she knew what it was like to have a phone super-glued to the ear.

But something made her hesitate. Maybe it was the serious expression on Liz's face. She punched in a number and waited, clearly listening to rings. When she got no answer, she put the phone down and glanced out the window again.

Nila recognized the expression. The girl was worried about something—so worried that it was affecting her work. What could cause a pretty local girl to seem so upset on such a lovely day?

And why should Nila care? After all, she was here to talk with Brody and Sydney Davis, and then she'd go back to Phoenix.

But once a reporter, always a reporter. Every little thing intrigued her. There was a story in the smallest worry.

Nila grinned at herself. Liz the waitress was probably wondering why her boyfriend hadn't called her or what time her date was for later that evening. Teenagers always blew things way out of proportion—and that was what Nila was in danger of doing if she wasn't careful.

She settled back into the booth and reviewed her notes. She had done a lot of research before coming to Roswell, and she had uncovered the reason for Brody Davis's reluctance to let his daughter speak with a reporter.

It seemed that Brody Davis had spoken to a few reporters himself, and the experience hadn't been a good one—at least for Davis. He was rich and obsessed by UFOs. So obsessed, in fact, that he claimed to have been abducted himself.

His obsession with aliens had brought him to Roswell

and led him to buy the UFO Center which, until Davis's purchase, had been little more than a cheesy museum for tourists—although the previous owner had, himself, been a believer.

Some people claimed that Brody Davis used the UFO Center as a cover for research he was doing into the entire phenomenon, and that he cared little for the museum part. He had an entire secret room in the back, filled with the latest equipment, most of it designed—depending on which source she read—for either protection against UFOs or calling them back to Earth.

When she'd initially called Davis, she hadn't known most of this, and so her promise not to do an interview had bordered on reportorial manipulation. But now, she knew, her series of features on the Christmas Miracle could be compromised by the mere presence of Brody Davis and his daughter, Sydney.

Nila had a hunch the two of them would remain deep background.

Liz brought her the vanilla shake and glanced curiously at Nila's laptop, but didn't say anything. She returned to the waitress station and picked up the phone again.

Nila frowned at her. Before she left, she'd ask what was going on, if she could figure out a way to do it. But she had more important things to concentrate on, such as a way to get the notoriously closed-mouthed Brody Davis to talk with her candidly.

She looked through the plate glass window. The UFO Center's quirky building was barely visible from her booth. It looked innocuous enough. She wondered how it would feel for poor Sydney to grow up as the only child of an eccentric rich man in a small town obsessed with UFOs.

Nila smiled. That was one question she wouldn't ask.

As she watched, she saw a blonde leave the UFO Center. The blonde stopped by a Jetta, opened the door, threw something inside, and then strode toward the Crashdown. As she got closer, her features came into perspective. She was pretty—not in the delicate way that Nila's waitress was—but in a pouty old-fashioned style that seemed to have gone out of vogue recently.

She was also younger than she had appeared initially, and she seemed as upset as the waitress had been.

The girl yanked open the Crashdown's door, and practically flung herself across the floor. Nila wasn't sure she'd ever seen anyone walk with such determination.

"Has he answered the phone?" Her voice carried across the diner.

"Maria!" Liz hung up the phone. She seemed surprised, and then her expression fell. "He wasn't there."

"And Brody hasn't seen him."

Nila's ears perked up at the mention of Brody's name.

"In fact," this Maria was saying, "Brody hasn't seen anyone for a while. He's been working on some new project. He's ordering special equipment and it's supposed to arrive in May. He's really excited about it and I couldn't get him to shut up long enough to answer any questions."

"So he doesn't know where Michael is?"

"No." Maria sat on one of the counter stools. "He said he didn't even know how to use his current equipment to check. He didn't even volunteer to help look, Liz. I thought he would, you know. He seems kind of—um—"

"Interested?" Liz said.

"Yeah." Maria nodded. "Interested."

Like Nila was. She continued to look at her computer screen while she watched out of the corner of her eye.

"That's why," Liz said. "I'll bet he'd be happy if Michael just left your life."

"You think?" Maria seemed buoyed by this news.

"Yeah, I do."

Maria sighed. "Has anyone else reported back yet?"

"Not yet," Liz said. "I tell you, this has been the hardest shift of my life. I'm having trouble concentrating. I've been forgetting orders and missing customers. You don't want to help, do you?"

"You think *you're* a mess," Maria said. "I do all of that on a good day."

Nila scrolled down her screen, wondering who Michael was and why they all cared that he was missing. And what Brody Davis had to do with all of it.

She would have to focus on Davis, anyway. She had more than enough questions for him. She wanted to know if he was anywhere near the room when the "angels" showed up.

She'd seen the angels. Two men in intern blue, walking down the hallway, having a heated conversation. Their movements, grainy and partially unfocused, had been caught by the hospital's security camera.

The whole thing had unfolded as a mini-drama, which had fascinated Nila the first time she saw it. The two men talking, then one of them disappearing into the room while the other stood watch. A nurse spoke to the remaining man, then left, coming back a short time later with the police. The man panicked, knocked on the door, and finally let himself inside, covering up the small window and blocking the door until he and his friend could make an escape.

The tape, it seemed to Nila, was the best proof that the guy on the Internet was running a scam. Both men had nothing in their hands as they walked down the hallway. They seemed agitated, almost as if they were arguing. And it was clear that the guy who stood outside the door was nervous.

If they had perpetrated a scam, using some kind of serum or something, then where had they carried it?

One of her follow-up questions to all of the parents had been whether or not the healing was permanent. She knew of some scams—very old scams—that used drugs which caused a quick sugar rush or a slight recovery that would disappear over time. Enough time had passed to make any false medication reveal itself.

So far, though, none of the children she'd found had relapsed. Which was good news. The strangest part of the whole thing, though, was the children's insistence that they'd seen an angel. And that the angel had left a silver handprint on their stomachs.

There was nothing about a silver handprint on the web site. When Nila returned to Phoenix, she would contact the police department and see if there was any record of that handprint. Sometimes, the police kept details of an event to themselves so that they could later use it to catch one of the perpetrators. The silver handprint seemed like one of those details.

A burger, stacked so high that it looked like it was about to topple over, appeared in front of her. Nila's stomach growled. She looked up as Liz set her ticket near the plate.

"It's just a formality," Liz said. "I'm a little distracted today."

"Yeah, I gathered that," Nila said. "Is something wrong?"

"One of our friends has disappeared," Liz said. "People are searching for him."

"How long has he been gone?" Nila asked.

"Since last night. No one knows where he is."

"Too soon to call the police, huh?" Nila said, trying to sound sympathetic.

Liz nodded.

"What's he look like? Maybe I've seen him."

At that moment, the door to the restaurant opened again and a short blonde entered. Liz's attention left Nila.

"Tess? Where's Max?"

"Parking," said the blonde. She tugged at her purse over her shoulder. Her hands were stained black, and she had a black streak on one cheek. "He'll be here in a minute."

"He wasn't there, was he?" Maria asked, as she came close.

"No," Tess said. "It doesn't look like anyone's been there for a long time."

"That's a good thing, right?" Liz remained near Nila's table. Tess gave her a measuring look.

Nila recognized it. The look two women gave each other when they wanted to be friends, but something was in the way—generally a man.

"Yeah," Tess said. "That's a good thing."

"Except for Michael." Maria peered out the door. "Something's happened to him."

"It's too soon to know that," Tess said.

Nila ate one of her fries. It was crispy and good, just like she suspected it would be. She continued to watch the three girls, wondering why there wasn't an adult involved in all of this. If a boy was missing—even a teenage boy—shouldn't an adult be as frantic as these girls were?

The frantic adult was probably out searching. That's what Nila would be doing if it were her son.

"Where did Max park? Siberia?" Maria asked.

"He's coming," Tess said. "Did you hear from anyone else?"

"Sheriff Valenti called a while ago," Liz said. "He hasn't heard anything."

"Kyle, Alex, and Isabel aren't back yet," Maria said.

"That's funny," Tess said. "They didn't have as far to go as we did."

Nila squished her burger with her fingers so that it would fit into her mouth. She took a big bite, and then moaned softly. She hadn't had a burger this good in years. She was glad she didn't live in this town. There didn't seem to be a lot of other restaurants that looked as good—and she didn't cook. She'd be wearing burger, fries, and shake on her hips in no time.

She continued to eat and scan her notes, while eavesdropping with half an ear. The girls were testy—Maria in particular, but Liz's voice had an edge whenever she spoke to Tess.

Finally, Maria said, "There's Max."

The door opened and Nila looked up.

Then she froze. She'd seen the handsome dark-haired

young man before. In fact, she had a digital copy of a surveillance tape with his face all over it.

He looked older and more comfortable in his blue
jeans and T-shirt, but it was clearly the same person.

Max, the girls had called him.

"No sign, I take it?" he said to Maria.

"None," she said.

"This isn't like him," Max said.

Liz went to his side. Tess bowed her head and stepped
back, making room. Interesting. So Nila had been right.
There was a boy between them, and it was this one, the
square-shouldered, strong-looking boy with a deep voice
and worried eyes.

"Everything was all right at the...um...?" Liz let her
voice trail off.

"Yeah," Max said. "Nothing unusual there."

And Nila had the odd sense he was talking about
something other than the missing boy. She glanced at
Tess, who surreptitiously wiped the black streak from her
face. The movement looked almost guilty.

What was going on here?

Nila's heart was pounding. She hadn't expected to find
anyone from the surveillance tape, not here in Roswell.
The scam's P.O. box was in Arizona.

She had to take this very carefully. The last thing she
wanted to do was frighten off any of these kids.

"You sound worried," Liz said to Max.

Max nodded. "Michael would have called in by now if
he could. You know that. He's gone off on his own before,
but he's never left us in the lurch like this, not without
knowing where he is."

Nila took a handful of fries, then pushed her plate away. Obviously Max and his friends lived in this town. She would have time to find out all she needed. If she didn't alienate anyone. If she was careful.

She finished her shake—it was too good to waste—and closed her laptop. She casually packed up her equipment so that no one could see what she had been doing.

"There's got to be something we missed," Max said. "Some kind of clue about where he is. People don't just vanish."

Yes, they did. They did all the time—usually on purpose. Nila saw it every day in her work. But she wasn't about to speak up and call attention to herself.

"We already checked the apartment," Liz said.

"But you were looking for him," Tess said. "You weren't looking to see what happened to him."

"That's true," Maria said, turning away from the window. "We didn't look that closely, Liz."

Liz nodded, her expression serious. Nila could tell she didn't like to be contradicted by Tess. Such undercurrents here.

Maybe they were all nervous because of the Christmas scam. Maybe they knew more than they were telling and they were worried for this Michael's health. They certainly seemed to be overreacting to the disappearance of a teenage boy who hadn't been gone a full day yet.

But they had said the sheriff was involved. That seemed even stranger, especially if they were involved in something illegal.

"I suppose we could go back to the apartment," Liz said. "There's probably stuff we missed."

"I'll go," Max said. "A fresh pair of eyes, and all that."

"Me, too," Tess said, a little too quickly.

Liz looked down, but not before Nila saw the annoyance in her expression.

Nila picked up her ticket.

"I'll drive," Maria said. "You don't mind, do you, Max?"

Nila stood. She wasn't far from them. She had decided. She'd play it the old-fashioned way.

"Still no luck with your friend, huh?" she asked Liz.

Liz shook her head.

"You know, sometimes people just go away for a while."

"I know," Liz said. She didn't seem as friendly as she had been a moment ago.

In fact, all of the teenagers had stiffened, as if Nila's questions made them nervous.

"Look," Nila said, her gaze meeting Max's. She almost took a step back. He had very powerful eyes. She hadn't expected that. She'd only seen that a few times—when she'd interviewed the governor, and when she'd met a rebel leader from South America, who was trying to raise funds for his guerrilla war.

Not crazy eyes. Just eyes that held a strength that most people couldn't claim.

"Yes?" he asked.

"I'm—ah," she caught herself sounding uncertain. She never sounded uncertain. It was bad for finding out information. "I was supposed to meet a man named Max Harris here about an hour ago. That's not you, is it?"

"No," he said.

She cursed silently. She shouldn't have asked the yes or no question. "I mean, because I heard them call you Max, and I just thought that with all that's going on, maybe you'd forgotten. Or decided that I'm not the person for the job and are trying to let me down easy by pretending not to show up."

She gave him a hopeful smile.

"I'm not Max Harris," he said.

"His last name is Evans," Liz said.

Tess glared at her, but no one else seemed upset. Then color flushed Liz's cheeks.

Why didn't anyone want Nila to know Max's last name? That intrigued her, but she didn't let the emotion show. "Do you know a Max Harris?" she asked them, hoping that they didn't, since she had made the name up on the spot.

"No." Tess's tone bordered on rude. She crossed her arms. "Isn't this a strange place for a job interview?"

"Not in the new economy," Nila said.

They all looked confused.

"I'm a consultant," Nila said, filling out her story. "Apparently, he works at home. I usually don't meet strange men in their homes. It's just safer this way."

Tess nodded, but she still looked suspicious. Maria hadn't been paying any attention at all. Liz's cheeks were still red. Max's strong gaze was still on Nila, as if he could see through her lies.

"Well," she said in a voice that was a little too cheerful. "Thanks for your help. I've got a few more meetings so I'm on my way. Good luck finding your friend."

"Thanks," Tess said, that undertone of hostility an overtone now.

Nila repressed the urge to give the girl a hard look,

then went to the counter to pay the bill. She had to wait for Liz, who rang her up without comment.

"I didn't mean to upset people," Nila said.

"You didn't," Liz said.

"I was just hoping that you knew Max Harris."

"I know," Liz said. "We're just…stressed. You know."

It sounded like an apology.

"I know," Nila said. "Thanks for everything."

And then she left, even though she didn't want to. She wanted to hang around and follow this Max Evans, wherever he was going. But she wasn't going to. She was going to see what she could learn about him and his family first. About his friends, about his connections to this town—and to Phoenix as well as other places in Arizona.

She was great at research. She'd find what she was looking for. Then she might follow Max Evans. Or she might interview him.

But not until she was ready.

Not until she knew more about him than he knew about himself.

"That was weird," Tess said. She crossed her arms and watched the petite woman walk down the sidewalk. The woman was staring at the UFO Center. "I don't like it."

"I don't either, but we have to focus on Michael," Max said.

"You shouldn't have told her Max's name," Tess said to Liz.

"I'm sorry," Liz said. "I wasn't thinking."

"She was fishing for it." Tess knew she was pushing too hard, but Liz was never cautious enough. If she had grown up on the run, like Tess had, always watching her back, she would know better than to blurt out things to strangers.

"It seemed that way, didn't it?" Max said, looking out the window, too.

Tess went outside and watched the woman get into a dusty sedan. It had Arizona license plates.

Max, Maria, and Liz came out and stood beside her.

"Do you think she has something to do with Michael's disappearance?" Maria asked.

"I have no idea," Max said.

"It's time to get an idea," Tess said. "I'm going to follow her."

"Tess," Max said.

"You can't. You're the one she's interested in. But I'm going to. Let me have your keys." She held out her hand. After a moment, Max handed her the keys to his Jeep.

She hurried down the street and got in, even as she heard Liz's voice behind her, apologizing to Max. Liz's voice grated on Tess, even though she tried hard not to let it. She didn't want it to grate. She wanted to get along.

She tried. Max had relationships that predated her— sort of, anyway. Relationships that were important to him. She had to respect them.

Most of the time. Except when the people in those relationships did something that might harm Max.

She turned the Jeep around and hurried down the road, narrowly missing a lime green VW bug, which honked loudly. Tess winced. She had a hunch Max would never let her drive his car again.

But she didn't care. She slipped into traffic, glad that

there wasn't much in this part of Roswell. She had a hunch she knew where the woman was going. Out-of-state plates driving in this direction generally had only one destination: Roswell's very tiny motel strip.

Sure enough, Tess caught sight of the sedan as it turned into the nicest chain hotel in Roswell. The woman parked, pulled out her purse and her heavy shoulder bag, and hurried inside.

Tess parked near the car, got out, and followed her.

The hotel's lobby still smelled of fresh paint. The place was new enough to have a not-lived-in look. The hotel clerk was an assistant coach at the high school. Tess didn't participate in sports, but the clerk seemed to recognize her. Her smile was warm.

"May I help you?"

"Yeah," Tess said, not sure yet what she was going to do. "Did you see a woman come through here just a minute ago?"

The clerk nodded. "The oh-so-important reporter? She's one of our guests."

Reporter? Tess felt a chill run down her back. "What do you mean, oh-so-important?"

The clerk shook her head. "She's made it clear since she arrived yesterday that everything has to be just so. She needs an extra line in her room for her modem. She expected to have a fax. She needed a current phone book. And she wanted to know everything there was to know about that weird guy at the UFO Center."

"Brody?" Tess asked.

The clerk nodded. "Do you want me to buzz her room?"

Tess frowned. "Um, no. She told me she was looking for a job. But I guess she's not, huh?"

"No." The clerk rolled her eyes. "She's from some Phoenix newspaper. Even showed me her credentials when she checked in, since they're paying the bill."

"Oh," Tess said. "My mistake, I guess."

The clerk frowned. "Kind of strange that she told you she was looking for a job. Is she investigating something?"

"I don't know," Tess said. "But she said she was meeting someone at the Crashdown for a consulting job interview."

"Maybe we should tell Brody," the clerk said.

Tess nodded. "That might be a good idea. What's her name?"

"Technically, I'm not supposed to tell you," the clerk said.

"I won't let anyone know where I got the information," Tess said. "In fact, you don't have to tell me if you want to call Brody yourself."

"No, I'd better not. Not from here, anyway." The clerk hit the keyboard on the computer below the desk. Tess heard the keys click. "Her name is Nila Spence. She's apparently a pretty big deal. Won some kind of award for investigative reporting."

That was precisely what Tess didn't want to hear. But she tried not to look too upset. "Thanks. I'll go see him right now."

"Probably a good idea," the clerk said as Tess left the hotel. Her breath was coming in short gasps, and she was more nervous than she thought.

She got into Max's Jeep and had trouble starting it, turning the ignition twice, and being rewarded with that horrible scrapey sound the engine made when it was already on. She wouldn't tell Max about that.

Then she backed out of her parking space and drove away quickly, hoping that Nila Spence wasn't looking out her fancy hotel window. She'd be wondering why one of the kids from the diner had followed her, and that would lead to more questions.

And more questions was exactly what they didn't need.

7

March 24—Scottsdale, Arizona

Michael's head still ached, but not as badly as before. His mouth tasted of cotton and stale socks. His entire body hurt in so many places that he couldn't separate them—except for the crick in his neck. He recognized that. It occurred whenever he fell asleep sitting up.

He brought his head up and opened his eyes. He did not expect what he saw—a very pink room, filled with stuffed animals and dolls.

He glanced around, moving his head slowly to ease the pain. A white toy chest covered with Barbie decals sat beneath a window with its frilly pink curtains drawn. Light was coming through those curtains, making the room look like the inside of a Pepto-Bismol bottle.

Michael blinked, letting his eyes focus. He was tied, his hands behind his back, his feet against chair legs. The ropes had been pulled so tight that his toes were falling asleep.

He sat for just a moment, getting his bearings. He

could get out of the ropes, but he wanted to figure out where he was first—and why he was there.

The room smelled of antiseptic and bubble gum. Raspy breathing, faint and uneven, came from the bed. As his eyes adjusted to the weird light, he saw a small figure on that bed, nearly lost beneath the pink comforter and lace canopy overhead.

A little girl, her face so pale as to be almost colorless, her eyes sunken deep into her head, her thin hands skeletal against the pillow.

Michael felt his heart lurch. He didn't like this at all.

A computer sat on a tiny white table near the other window. Child-size chairs were pulled up beneath it. Next to the computer was something that looked like a walkie-talkie, but it had the image of a baby on it. Another walkie-talkie contraption sat on the end table beside the bed, next to a pink lamp with a ballerina for a base.

A man sat on a rocking chair near the bed. He was clutching a picture book between his large hands, but he wasn't reading it. Instead, he was staring at the little girl.

The man wasn't tied up. He didn't seem to be imprisoned. In fact, the door to the bedroom was open, and through it, Michael could see sunlight falling across the hallway carpet. Far away, a phone rang four times, so faint that he could barely hear it.

Obviously, the man didn't even notice because he didn't move.

The little girl didn't seem to be able to move, either.

Michael glanced at the windows. Two of them at angles to each other. A corner room with good lighting. There was a door near one of the windows, but it was partially open, revealing impossibly tiny clothes and shoes hanging inside.

The only door into the room was behind the man in the rocking chair.

Michael tugged on the ropes. If he eased them off his wrists, then got them off his feet without attracting attention, he'd still have to figure which way out was the best—the windows or the door.

He didn't like either option.

He felt someone looking at him. He turned toward the bed. The man was staring at him. The man was younger than he'd seemed from the side—maybe ten years older than Michael—but his mouth was lined, and he had bags under his eyes.

"Sorry about hitting you," the man said.

"What?" Michael said. The guy was apologizing for kidnapping him?

"And I'm sorry about drugging you, too, but I couldn't guarantee that you'd come with me."

"You could have tried asking," Michael said, fury rising up within him. He hadn't really been angry until now. Dazed yes, but not angry. He hadn't known what was going on.

"I suppose," the guy said, "but it probably would have sounded crazy to you."

"Maybe," Michael said, "but I doubt I would have preferred getting hit on the head. That hurt, you know?"

"Shh," the man said, putting a finger to his lips. "Please don't wake Katie. She's having a tough enough time of it as it is."

"What's wrong with her?" Michael asked, and then

wished he hadn't. He didn't want to know. He didn't want to be involved with this crazy man or his schemes. It was time to break off the bonds and hurry out the door.

But he didn't. Not yet. This was just too weird.

"They don't know," the guy was saying. "That's why I had to find you."

The sentence made Michael's stomach clench. He closed his eyes.

"I'm pissed about what happened last night," he had said to Max the day after they'd driven to Phoenix.

Max had sighed and looked at his family's Christmas tree. The house had been festive, just like it always was. Like Michael's house, be it the trailer or his apartment, had never been.

"Michael," Max had said. "I couldn't . . . stop myself."

"No, no, no," Michael had said, not quite looking Max in the face. "I'm pissed that I don't have the ability to help the kids in the hospital that you couldn't get to."

And now he was facing one, he just knew it. Him, not Maxwell. Michael, the guy without the right skills. It always came down to that.

He made himself open his eyes. "Find me for what?"

The guy shook his head. "It seemed so clear the other day, before I got the e-mail."

Oh, great. The guy really was crazy.

"What seemed clear?"

"I saw you in the hospital the night the children got saved. You missed Katie. She was in intensive care." The guy put his hand on Katie's bed, not quite touching her.

Intensive care. Michael's mouth went dry.

He stared at the bed and the young girl barely visible there. She was so sick, she probably was going to die.

She'd been that sick since Christmas. And they'd missed her. They hadn't been able to help her because they didn't even know she was there.

"I don't know what you think I can do," Michael said, sounding as defensive as he felt.

The man put his hands through his hair. "I wanted you to show me how you healed the others. Did you use a serum or a pill or was it something else? Did you have help? I know you knocked on that door, warning someone. What was that person doing? Was it the serum?"

"Serum?" Michael asked. "What serum?"

The guy stood, shoving his hands into his back pockets. His restlessness made Michael restless as well.

"The serum I just paid fifteen grand for. The stuff that they say healed the kids."

Michael stiffened. "Who says?"

"The web site."

"What web site?"

"The one about the serum."

They were getting nowhere. And it sounded like someone was trying to take credit for Max's actions.

"Tell me about it," Michael said. He wasn't going to leave until he knew exactly what was going on.

"I saw you," the guy said. He was close to the chair now. He wasn't that tall or that big. Even without his powers, Michael could take him. "At the hospital, in the hallway. I'd come out of Katie's room, and I saw you standing there. I saw the nurse bring the cops, saw you warn whoever was inside, and then I saw the kids. I know you're not an angel. I know you did something—

you and the people who helped you. I want to know what it is."

The guy wasn't very focused. "I want to know about the serum," Michael said.

"I'm a dot-com millionaire," the guy said, almost to himself. "I sold all my stock when my wife got sick. Who knew that I'd be one of the few guys who'd make a profit in the market?"

"The serum," Michael said.

"I was getting to that." The guy paced. He stopped near one of the windows, but he didn't pull the curtain open. Instead, he just stood, with his back to Michael. "I have the time, you see. I could sit with Katie when she got ill, and I could try to figure out what happened in that room. The kids—they got better, really better. None of them relapsed."

Of course not, Michael thought. Max had absorbed the sickness, then thrown it away. He'd been sick himself afterward—sick and without his powers for days.

"So I knew whatever happened was real. No one took credit for it, which I thought was strange. The police released your sketch."

Michael started. Great. There was a sketch of him somewhere.

"But," the guy continued, "no one recognized you—and the police never said that the sketch was tied to the healings. Didn't want to mess with the Christmas Miracle, I guess."

Michael stayed very still. He didn't want to break the guy's train of thought.

"The kids kept insisting they saw an angel, but I knew you were real. And there was other evidence, like that open window and the footprints on the ground outside. The nurse had seen you, and she said there was someone else with you. She wasn't really sure how many people were in that room that night. She was convinced that a miracle happened, but people don't make miracles. They make medicine or try experimental treatments. Miracles don't happen."

Yes, they do, Michael wanted to say. *You should just see my friend Max.* But he stayed silent.

The guy bowed his head. "So I tried to trace you. First, I talked to all the parents of all the kids. Katie was still in the hospital then, so I managed a trip to Roswell. I saw you flipping burgers in that diner."

"The Crashdown," Michael said, figuring that wouldn't give him away.

"Yeah," the guy said. "And I was stunned. I figured if you had the ability to save kids, you wouldn't be flipping burgers."

Brilliant deduction, Sherlock. Michael literally bit his tongue to keep from saying everything he was thinking. The pain kept him alert.

"So I figured you were just helping somebody. You know, maybe you were the driver or the lookout."

Michael shook his head. The guy still had his back to him, though, and couldn't see it.

"I followed you home, but I wasn't ready then."

"Ready for what?" Michael asked.

"I didn't know how I'd use you."

Michael let out an exasperated sigh. "Use me for what?"

"To save Katie."

The guy turned. His voice had risen slightly, and his cheeks were flushed.

Michael could feel his desperation.

"What does this have to do with some serum?" Michael asked, trying to keep the guy focused. He'd find out about this serum and then he'd leave.

"I came back here—I didn't dare be away from Katie much longer, and—"

"Where's here?" Michael asked, with a sinking feeling. He had a hunch he knew.

"Scottsdale."

Right outside of Phoenix. Seven-plus hours from Roswell. Just like Michael had expected. No wonder the guy had him drugged and out cold.

And in the trunk of a car, like a piece of luggage.

The anger that Michael had been holding back rose again. He clenched his teeth, trying to stay calm just for a moment or two longer.

"When you came back, what did you do?" Michael asked.

"I was searching the web for medical information. They thought Katie had some super virus at the time, and I was afraid they were right, so I was looking up every-thing about it, when I saw the web site."

"The web site?" That's right. Keep him talking.

"Yeah," the guy said. "It talked about the serum, and how your friends had tried to get FDA approval, but it hadn't worked because the FDA is in league with the major drug companies and those companies don't want an all-purpose drug like this one on the market. It'll cut into their profits."

"You believed that crap?"

"No, not really."

The guy hunched his shoulders forward. "But Katie's so sick. I can't afford to ignore things. So I read the site. And it talked about how they went to the hospital in Phoenix at Christmas and used the medication on the children there to prove that it worked. Still the FDA denied them—"

"I can't believe this!" Michael said.

The guy stopped and swallowed so hard that his Adam's apple bobbed.

Michael clenched his fists behind his back. He had to stay calm. He had to. Otherwise he wouldn't find out what this guy knew.

"You don't know about them, do you?" the guy asked quietly.

"What else did the web site say?" Michael asked.

The guy licked his lips. He glanced at Katie on the bed, then back at Michael. "It said that because they couldn't get government approval, they decided to give the stuff away themselves, with a slight donation. It's not entirely legal, so there are a bunch of hoops to go through."

"How much did the hoop cost you?" Michael asked.

"Fifteen thousand dollars. Cash."

"Come on," Michael said. "Even I know better than to send cash to some people with nothing more than a web site and a stupid story."

He could almost imagine what Maria would say about the whole thing, after she stopped laughing in that cute way of hers.

"Maybe you do," the guy said softly. "But you don't have a daughter with a disease that no one understands.

You haven't run out of options yet. I can afford to lose fifteen thousand on a gamble like this."

"So where's the stuff?"

"I have to pick it up today."

"Then what did you kidnap me for?"

The guy looked at him. "I thought that they weren't going to answer me. I'd sent the money and I hadn't heard back from them. So I decided I'd get you. You could tell me where they were, and if they weren't the guys, then you could tell me who was. You know what happened in that room."

Yes, he did, and he wasn't about to tell this man. Although he wished Max were here. If Max were here, they could save this poor little girl, and figure out how to deal with her weird father together.

At that moment, the little girl moaned. The man turned so fast that Michael thought he was going to fall over. He sat on the edge of Katie's bed and took her hand.

"How're you feeling, sweetheart?" he asked.

"Thirsty." Katie's voice was as raspy and tired as her breathing.

"I'll get you some ice," the man said.

"I want Kool-Aid, Daddy."

"Ice first," the man said. "The doctor said it was easier for you to swallow."

He left the room, almost at a sprint. The little girl leaned against the pillow and closed her eyes. She hadn't even noticed Michael.

Michael stared at her for a long time. He'd seen how those kids had looked in that hospital ward before Max had touched them, and how they looked after. She looked worse than the kids had that night.

This wasn't fair. None of it was fair. No wonder Max hadn't stopped that night.

Michael would get up and help her, if he could. If he had the power.

He could hear rattling in the kitchen. This was his chance. He could get away now.

The little girl moaned again, and Michael wondered if she was in pain.

So someone was claiming that a serum had healed those kids. Someone was running a scam on all that Max had done. Michael's anger grew.

Who knew what that $15,000 serum really did to sick kids like poor Katie here. Maybe it was harmless. But maybe it killed the kids. Maybe it just made them sicker.

He wasn't going to leave until he knew where this guy was going to go to pick up the serum. Michael would stop those crooks from making a buck off Max's kindness, off little kids' lives.

And then he would find Max. Max could help Katie.

So maybe the crazy guy's gamble was paying off. Michael was going to do what the guy wanted him to do—but not for the reasons the guy thought.

Because Michael couldn't stand the way that poor little girl looked, so lost in her own bed. He couldn't stand to hear her labored breathing, and see her pale face.

He knew, just like he had known at Christmas, that she was only one of many. But she was the one before him.

And, like Max, Michael had to help—no matter what.

8

"A reporter?" Maria asked. She was having trouble wrapping her mind around all of this because her worry for Michael was growing as each hour passed.

Now there was a new twist. A reporter had lied to them. Why?

Maria was sitting at the back booth at the Crashdown. Max was leaning against the edge of the booth and Liz was beside him, looking upset. Tess had just finished telling them about her trip to the hotel.

"I don't understand," Liz said. "Why would a reporter say she was looking for a job when she wasn't?"

"She was up to something." Tess glanced at Max. He wasn't looking at her. He was watching Liz with that intense look he'd had ever since they met him. "She wanted to know your last name."

"You don't know that," Max said.

"You think she really was waiting for some guy named

93

Max Harris?" Tess walked over to the counter and went behind it as if she worked in the place. She grabbed the phone book and started thumbing through it. "There are a lot of Harrises here. You want me to start calling them to see if there's a Max?"

Maria knew, as well as the others did, that it wouldn't do any good. "Why is this happening now? We should be focused on finding Michael."

"Maybe the two things are related," Max said.

"Michael's disappearance and her interest in you?" Liz asked.

Max nodded. "Have there been any other strange people around lately?"

"Some guy in a suit last night," Liz said. "He asked Maria out."

"He did not," Maria said.

"Yes, he did," Liz said. "A number of times. You kept turning him down because you were waiting for Michael."

"He wasn't serious," Maria said.

"He sounded serious to me."

"A guy in a suit?" Max asked. "Why is that strange?"

"I'd never seen him before," Liz said.

"He didn't look local," Maria said.

Tess had closed the phone book. "How can someone not look local?"

"I think it was something he said." Maria grabbed the salt shaker and slid it back and forth between her hands. "Something about what's there to do at night in Roswell."

"It was a pickup line," Tess said.

"Yeah, but he would have used a different one if he'd been from here," Maria said.

At that moment, Sheriff Valenti came into the Crashdown. Maria still had a hard time thinking of him as anything but the sheriff, even though his deputy, Hanson, was now in charge. Valenti, for all his wiry strength and easy manner, seemed more in control, more powerful than all the others.

Tess set down the phone book and hurried toward him. "Find anything?"

Valenti shook his head. "I even checked the apartment again, looking for things that weren't obvious. There were some footprints in the bushes, but I can't tell you if they're new, old, or even important."

The door to the restaurant opened again, and some customers entered. Liz sighed. The place had been slow for hours, but even a handful of customers was distracting for her. Another waitress was on duty, but Maria should probably put on her uniform and help—only she didn't want to.

Then Kyle and Alex came in, heads bowed, conversing softly. Tess moved closer to them, close to Kyle, like she always did. She was clearly interested in Kyle. Anyone with eyes could see that—except Liz, of course, who believed that Tess wanted nothing and no one but Max.

"Nothing in the woods?" Maria asked.

Alex shook his head. He came toward the booth and gave her a reassuring smile. She could tell that he was worried, although probably not as worried as she was.

No one was as worried as she was.

Sure, she knew that Michael could handle himself. She'd seen him, with his so-called family, with the Skins. She knew that he had powers and wasn't afraid to use them. But she also knew the toll they took on him emotionally and how fragile Michael really was under that tough-guy exterior.

Who could have gotten to him? And why?

She wished she'd been able to convince him to carry a phone like a normal person. At least then she could have tried to call him—even if it meant listening to the phone ring over and over again.

"Where's Isabel?" Max asked.

Kyle's gaze met Alex's.

Maria's stomach flip-flopped. The mysterious "they" hadn't gotten Isabel, too, had they?

She could see the same reaction on Max's face.

"She, um..." Kyle started, then looked to Alex for help.

Alex closed his eyes. Somehow distasteful tasks always seemed to fall on his shoulders. Maria knew he resented it, but he was so helpful all the time. He was such an essential part of their group that he was often noticed only when he was absent—like he had been earlier in the year on that exchange program. Suddenly there wasn't Alex to lean on anymore, and that had been disconcerting.

"She, um..." Kyle said again, and waited, as if he just couldn't bring himself to say what was next.

"She what?" Max leaned toward Kyle, the tension between them palpable.

Alex sighed and opened his eyes. "She went home to get something of Michael's. She's afraid that the only way we're going to be able to find him is through extraterrestrial means."

Max's face paled. He nodded once, then looked away.

"What do you think we should do?" Liz asked Valenti.

He shook his head. "Missing persons are the hardest cases of all."

Missing persons. Maria felt herself go cold. Michael's disappearance had an official label now.

"I guess," Valenti continued, "we just keep looking."

"Maybe we should look for that guy in the suit," Max said.

"He was here when Michael disappeared," Maria said. It felt as if she were talking through cotton. She had to focus, had to think. It wasn't doing Michael any good for her to be so shaken up. "He couldn't have had anything to do with it."

"That's right," Liz said. "Besides, he ate at the diner real early this morning, and I saw him drive off. He had a suit in his car, and he'd opened his trunk to put something in it. Only luggage."

"Where was the car from?" Valenti asked. "Maybe we should check anyway."

Liz shrugged. "It had New Mexico plates. But there was a bumper sticker about Albuquerque on it."

"If you remember the plate number, I might be able to check it out."

Liz frowned. She wrote something on one of the tickets and handed it to Valenti.

At one of the tables, the new customers waved their menus like a surrender flag.

Liz cursed and hurried toward them.

"I really don't think it was him," Maria said.

"Doesn't hurt to check," Valenti said.

"Then maybe you should check on the reporter, too," Max said.

"Reporter?"

Tess explained what happened that afternoon.

"That sounds a lot more interesting than this guy in the suit," Kyle said.

"Yeah," Alex said. "Why would a reporter be here now?"

"That's what I was wondering," Maria said.

"She was looking at pictures of Brody when I waited on her." Liz had come back. She was clutching her ticket book in her hand. She hadn't put the customers' order up yet or gotten their drinks.

"Brody?" Maria asked. "Why?"

Liz shrugged. "She had them on a laptop. And she was making notes."

"I don't like it," Max said.

"All right," Valenti said. "We'll check her out, too."

"And no one talk to her," Max said.

"You didn't have to tell us that." Tess gave him a fond smile. "It's obvious."

Liz rolled her eyes and walked away.

Maria rubbed her hands on her jeans. She needed a plan, and she couldn't come up with one. They knew what they *weren't* supposed to do, but not what they *were* supposed to do.

"So what happens now?" Maria asked. "Do we sit and wait or is there somewhere else to look?"

No one met her gaze, and no one answered her. They all seemed as uncertain about this as she was.

And she didn't like it.

None of them did.

Maxwell Evans's school records were fascinating. Nila Spence had found them during an Internet search. Max was younger than she thought. The power of those eyes made her think he was around twenty, when he was actually still in high school.

From her Internet search, she had discovered that he went to Roswell High, and from there, she was able to hack into the high school's computer system.

Max was an exceptional student, even though he missed class more than he should have—a problem that had grown in the past two years as his friendship with other members of his class, Maria DeLuca and Tess Harding, had grown.

He'd also had a rocky love life, as evidenced by the current guidance counselor's notes. He'd become close to a Liz Parker—who had to be the Liz of the Crashdown—and had nearly come to blows with her former boyfriend, Kyle Valenti, the sheriff's son. The current counselor believed that Max's relationship with Liz caused many of his problems this year, as well as the bad influence of one of the poorer students in the class—a Michael Guerin.

Apparently, Michael Guerin was the boy who was missing. Guerin, who came from a troubled home, had had the state rule him an adult, even though he was only seventeen. Shortly thereafter, his troublemaking father had been murdered outside of Roswell. According to newspaper accounts, which Nila had looked up, Guerin was not considered a suspect.

The most fascinating information in Max's file came from the previous guidance counselor, a Miss Topolsky. Her early notes were quite detailed, but her later ones became very cryptic. Most of her work focused on Max and his sister, Isabel—a straight-A student who was well loved by her teachers.

Apparently, this Miss Topolsky thought that these two were unusually gifted and for some reason that made her nervous. She felt that they needed to be watched.

She also made a lot of notes about Liz Parker, a science wiz whose interest in Max struck Topolsky as unusual. Nila hadn't gotten that sense, but then there was no mention in Topolsky's notes about Tess Harding.

Perhaps Tess had come later.

There were also some local newspaper mentions of Max. At first they were the typical articles newspapers featured about gifted students: he had excelled at a spelling bee in the sixth grade; he had placed second in a middle school debate contest, that sort of thing. But the later articles were strange.

The most recent, which came from last fall, simply stated that the FBI had spoken with Max and Isabel Evans regarding their connections to fired sheriff Jim Valenti, which then led to an entire slew of articles about the firing of the sheriff and the strange case that led up to it.

She couldn't really get a handle on what he had done

wrong. He had supposedly threatened a witness or harassed someone or had brought the teenagers to a crime scene where they didn't belong. Depending on who the paper interviewed, the story changed.

There were no interviews with former Sheriff Valenti, Max Evans, or his sister, Isabel. The current sheriff had no comment, and neither did the FBI agent who worked the case.

Nila stared at those documents for a long time. Something strange was happening in Roswell and it had spilled over to Phoenix just before Christmas.

Somehow Max had been involved. So had Michael Guerin. The paper ran his picture when he divorced his family and became a legal adult. She recognized the face as belonging to the nervous young man who stood outside the door, waiting for Max Evans to complete whatever he did in that pediatric ward.

Was this why Michael Guerin had disappeared? Did it have something to do with the Phoenix incident? Was that why Max Evans had seemed so nervous?

Clearly these teenagers weren't major players in the serum sales scam over the Internet. If they were, they wouldn't be working menial jobs like Liz Parker was. They would be spending the money, as teenagers did.

Maybe Guerin's disappearance was tied to the serum sale. Maybe these kids had been a front for the scam. But that didn't make sense. All of the children had been healed—and stayed healed. Nila didn't have to see the children who received the serum from the Internet scam to know they hadn't gotten any better—although she would try to find some of them, too. She always double-and triple-checked her sources.

It was the only way to be a journalist, no matter what those idiots on TV did.

One of the articles mentioned that Max worked at the UFO Center—at least he had a while ago. Which meant he probably knew Brody Davis.

It couldn't be coincidence that four people from the same town had ended up in the Phoenix hospital that night—Brody and Sydney Davis, Michael Guerin and Max Evans. Maybe if she found the link between all of them, she would have the missing piece of the puzzle.

The thought of Brody Davis made her check the clock on her computer. It was nearly time for her interview with him.

She grabbed her purse and her Palm Pilot, but opted to leave her laptop in the room. She didn't want to scare him away.

Then she hurried down the stairs and out the side exit to her car.

Roswell was an easy city to navigate—if calling it a city was even accurate. She decided to take the long route to the UFO Center. She wanted to drive past the Evans's house, see where Max and his sister lived.

Nila wasn't sure what she was looking for. A reporter's daydream, of course, would be to see if the family lived way above its means. Maybe the parents were involved in this somehow.

Although she doubted she'd find anything as easy as that. But it wouldn't hurt to look.

She drove quickly through the narrow streets, and

slowed when she reached the Evans's block. None of the houses looked out of place. The Evans's house was trim and neat, but not expensive.

As Nila watched, a tall blond woman came out the front door. She carried herself like a ballet dancer—straight spine, graceful movements—and it wasn't until she came down the porch steps that Nila realized she was looking at Isabel Evans.

Max's sister, like Max, had a poise that made her seem older than she was.

The girl was walking quickly toward a car parked in the driveway. Nila made a hasty decision.

She pulled up and parked on the street, blocking the driveway. Isabel looked at her, and for a moment, Nila thought she saw fear on Isabel's face.

"Are you Isabel Evans?" Nila asked as she got out of the car.

"Who wants to know?" Isabel asked. Her voice was rich and smooth, calmer than her eyes were. If Nila hadn't seen her uncomfortable look, she would have thought the girl was fine.

"My name is Nila Spence. I'm an investigative journalist from Phoenix."

Isabel didn't flinch. But she didn't move either.

"I'm tracing a scam," Nila said. "People are selling a fake serum, supposedly guaranteed to heal many childhood diseases."

"Sounds awful." Even though Isabel's comment was designed to be perfunctory, there was compassion in her voice.

The compassion took Nila by surprise.

"The people who are selling the serum claim they caused a Christmas miracle at a local Phoenix hospital. They claim they saved the lives of more than a dozen children who were dying of cancer."

Isabel swallowed and something too strong to be fear passed through her eyes. "Really?"

"I know your brother was at the hospital on the night of December twenty-fourth. I also know that he locked himself in the Pediatric Oncology ward."

Isabel raised perfectly plucked eyebrows.

"Selling drugs through the mail is a federal offense, Ms. Evans, punishable by decades in prison. The government doesn't discriminate between street drugs and drugs that are supposedly used to do good. If the drugs are illegal, then the sellers are prosecuted to the full extent of the law."

Isabel put her hands behind her back. Her movement made it clear that she was taller than Nila.

Nila got that same sense of power she had felt from Max. It was odd, really. She'd interviewed dozens of teenagers over the years, and none of them had made her feel as if she were the one at a disadvantage.

"I know your brother is mixed up in this somehow," she said. "I can keep his name out of it if he's willing to talk to me."

Isabel was just staring at her, face impassive, as if she were listening, but not feeling anything.

Nila reached into her purse and pulled out a business card. On it, she had written the number at the hotel as well as her cell phone number.

"Have him call me," she said. "I'll be at this number until tomorrow."

She extended the card toward Isabel, who stared at it for a long moment before taking it. Then, without waiting for an answer, Nila returned to her car and drove off.

Nila was shaking, with exhilaration and from nerves. She felt like she finally had a direction in her research.

Unfortunately, she wasn't certain in which direction she was actually going.

9

March 24—Roswell, New Mexico

Max took a bite out of his hamburger. He felt guilty eating—he should have been out looking for Michael—but he hadn't eaten all day. As Liz pointed out, he needed to keep up his strength. What she didn't say was he needed to keep it up in case he had to use it.

Sheriff Valenti had gone home to see if he could call in some favors and find out more about the reporter. Alex had decided to go to the high school, which was one of the few places no one had checked. Kyle had gone with his father.

Tess wanted to stay with Max. Liz had seemed annoyed when she heard that, but she hadn't said anything. They weren't together anymore, and it was her choice. Her gaze still met his at the most inopportune moments, and he felt like he could see right through her.

See through her and no longer understand her. He still felt the pull between them. He knew she did too, yet she insisted they stay apart. Sometimes it made sense to him—especially when he thought about his destiny, about the granilith and all that had happened in the past two years. But sometimes it made no sense at all. Being in love was easy; the two people who loved each other had to be together.

It was hard to realize that life didn't work that way.

Maria was still sitting in the booth, using her cell phone. She was calling everyone she knew, and everyone Michael knew, hoping they had seen him. She had reached her mother first, hoping that for some reason, Michael was there.

He wasn't, of course. And her weird cousin Sean had volunteered to help. Maria had turned him down, saying he was quite the screw-up and she didn't want his help.

Surprisingly, it had been Liz who had argued with her. Liz, whom he had caught tickling and goofing with Sean some time ago. She was attracted to him. Max knew that as clearly as he knew his own name.

Not that he had any say in it. They weren't a couple.

It seemed like he had to remind himself of that every few minutes just so that he could believe it.

"Max!"

He turned. Isabel was coming toward him, a look of panic on her face. The other customers stared at her. Liz and Maria hurried to her side. Tess stayed beside Max, saying nothing.

Max didn't move. Isabel had gone to get something of Michael's so that they would get a sense of him. Maybe she knew something. And with that expression on her face, whatever it was couldn't be good.

"Come sit down, Isabel," he said.

She didn't pay much attention to Liz or Maria. Her entire gaze was for him.

"Max," she said as she sat beside him. "Do you know there's a reporter in town?"

"Yes. She was here a little while ago."

Isabel set a business card next to the Tabasco bottle. "She wants to talk with you, Max. She knows you were in Phoenix at Christmas."

He felt all the muscles in his back tense. "How does she know that?"

"She wouldn't tell me. But she knew that you were in that children's ward, and she knew the kids got better."

"I knew something was up with her," Tess said softly beside him.

Maria and Liz flanked him.

"She wants to talk with you," Isabel said. "She thinks you're involved in some kind of drug-dealing scam."

"Max?" Liz gave a half-laugh of surprise. "Max is the last person who would ever deal drugs."

Isabel shook her head. "Someone is. They're claiming credit for saving the kids and selling some fake drug, saying it was the reason the kids got better."

"What?" That news seemed to bring Maria out of her funk. "Of all the low-down, nasty, *creepy* things to do."

"Are they selling this drug saying it'll make other kids better?" Liz asked.

"I guess so," Isabel said. "At least, that's what I understood."

Max felt a fury run through him. He hadn't felt anything like this since that afternoon he'd faced the Skins.

He pushed his plate away, took a deep breath to keep

control of himself, and made sure he could sound calm before he spoke.

"What does she want from me?"

"I don't know," Isabel said. "She just wants to talk with you."

"What did you tell her?"

"Nothing," Isabel said. "I just listened. She apparently didn't care if I responded or not."

"Where did you see her?" Tess asked.

"At the house," Isabel said.

"She knows where we live?" She hadn't seemed like that much of a threat when Max had seen her.

"I guess so." Isabel pushed a strand of hair out of her face. "I guess she was waiting for one of us. She parked in front of me when she saw me."

"Good thing she didn't see Mom and Dad first," Max said.

"Yeah," Isabel said. "Mom talked about that miracle for nearly a week."

"It was Christmas, after all." Max kept his voice dry. He'd hated listening to his mother go on and on about a real miracle. He'd wanted to confide in her so much, and he had been unable to.

This past Christmas had been the hardest holiday of his life.

Tess put her hand on his shoulder. It was meant as a gesture of support, but it made him uncomfortable. He saw Liz's eyes flash and had to look away.

"Did she know Michael was there, too?" Max made sure he spoke so softly that no one outside their group could hear him.

"I don't know," Isabel said. "The conversation was pretty short."

"This can't be a coincidence." Maria's voice carried more than Max wanted it to. "Maybe she knows where Michael is."

"Reporters don't kidnap people," Tess said.

"I didn't say that." Maria wasn't even pretending to be civil to anyone anymore. "I said maybe she knows where he is."

"You know," Liz said in that considered way of hers. "Maybe Michael found out about this scam."

"And he went off to do something about it." Isabel turned toward Liz. It was plain they both believed this was a possibility.

Max frowned. It *was* a possibility.

"That would be so like him," Maria said with a mixture of pride and exasperation. "Running off without telling anyone, trying to be the hero—"

"We don't know what happened," Max said gently.

"But this is likely, Max," Maria said. "It's the first thing."

"It is." Max shook his head. "But it doesn't feel right. How would he have found out in the three hours between the time I last saw him and you first called?"

"I don't know. Maybe someone came to see him." Maria crossed her arms.

"Like that reporter," Isabel said. "Maybe she saw him last night."

"And he just ran off without calling anyone?" Max looked at all of them. They were watching him intently. "He didn't call me or you, Maria, even though he knew you were waiting for him? Or you, Isabel? Whenever he feels he can't confide in me, he at least tells you."

"Maybe he didn't have time," she said. "Maybe he just had to go."

"And why would that be?" Max asked. "What would be the hurry?"

"I don't know." Isabel stood up quickly. He recognized the move. She did that when she was irritated with him. "It just seems like something Michael would do."

Max didn't agree. Michael would come to him. The only time Michael went off on his own was when he was really angry with Max, and they'd had a pleasant afternoon together, talking basketball. It was like old times.

Michael would have called.

"Maybe you should see the reporter," Liz said.

Everyone turned toward her.

"You've got to be kidding," Tess said.

Liz shook her head. "I'm not kidding. It sounds like she knows stuff we don't. Maybe Max can find out what's really going on."

"And maybe she'll ask the wrong questions. Or maybe she's not a reporter at all," Isabel said.

"She's a reporter," Tess said. "She used some newspaper credentials for her hotel room."

"If she asks the wrong questions," Max said, "I just won't answer."

"Oh, like that will work." Isabel sighed. "She's probably already suspicious because I didn't deny your involvement. I couldn't think of what to say. I figured if I said anything I put us all in trouble. And that's what'll happen if you go to see her, Max."

"I can handle myself."

"You don't know that. You don't know who or what she is." Isabel took his hand. "Michael's already missing. I don't want anything to happen to you, too."

Liz's eyes seemed to get bigger. Maria was watching both of them.

But it was Tess who spoke. "You're going to go, aren't you?"

"Yes," Max said. He wondered how she could read him so clearly. She'd been able to since they'd met.

"Then I'll go with you," she said.

"What purpose will that serve?" Maria asked. This time it was clear to Max that she was asking the question for Liz.

"If the reporter asks the wrong question and Max gives the wrong answer, maybe I can muddy things up a bit."

Tess was talking about her power, the way that she made people believe they saw something or heard something that didn't really happen.

"Can you do that after the fact?" Isabel asked.

"Not exactly, but I can be pretty creative."

"All right, then," Max said. "I'll go and Tess will come with me."

"And what about the rest of us?" Maria asked. "I can't stay in this diner any longer. I have to do something."

"We can't all go see the reporter," Isabel said. "That would really make her suspicious."

"I wasn't really thinking about that reporter," Maria said. "I was thinking about Michael. What do we do about Michael?"

Isabel held up a neck chain that Max recognized. Michael had worn it for a while years ago, and then it broke. Isabel had promised to fix it, but apparently she hadn't gotten around to it.

"Maybe we can focus on him, and get a sense of him."

Maria shook her head. "I've got to act, Isabel. I can't use my nonexistent powers. What I do well is talk and move. That's about it."

"You sing pretty well," Liz said.

"You know what I mean," Maria said.

"I do." Liz wiped her hands on her uniform. "I'm going to see if I can get the rest of the shift off. Then we'll go to Michael's place."

"The sheriff's already been there," Tess said.

"Yes, but he's not familiar with it," Liz said. "We are. We can see if anything's out of place."

"Everything's out of place," Isabel said.

They would argue all day if they weren't careful. "I think it's a good idea," Max said. "The more things we try, the better chance we have of finding him."

"He should have turned up by now," Maria said, her gaze meeting Max's.

"Yes," Max said. "He should have. That's why I think we should do everything we can to find him. We all know that something's wrong. We just have to find out what."

Isabel threaded her hands through her hair. "Do you guys ever have the feeling that everything is going to change? By summer, we're not even going to recognize ourselves and our lives?"

"Don't talk like that, Isabel," Max said.

She didn't look at him. "I do. I have a feeling that we aren't going to want to go through this spring. That we'll look back on the winter, and wish it were still here."

"Isabel, this isn't helping," Max said. She was actually scaring him.

"Yeah," Liz said. "I feel that way sometimes."

"Me, too," Maria said.

"Great," Tess said. "Now that we're all depressed, can we get out of here?"

She looked at Max. His stomach turned. The hamburger wasn't sitting well.

Isabel was right. Things were changing in ways he couldn't see yet. But somehow he had a feeling the upcoming changes had nothing to do with Michael's disappearance.

Max had a growing sense that Michael's disappearance was rooted in the past—and Isabel's feelings had their place in the future.

"We'll find you guys," Max said, and stood. He led Tess out of the Crashdown before anyone could protest.

Before he could change his mind.

"Nothing." Maria flopped on Michael's couch and then winced when the broken spring scraped her leg. "There's nothing here."

"I can't believe how messy this place is." Isabel stood in the kitchen, her nose wrinkled. The smell was pretty incredible. After a few days, leftover pizza took on a life of its own.

"I don't know what we expected to find, anyway," Liz said. She had changed out of her uniform into the camisole T-shirt and jeans she had worn that morning. "We looked earlier."

"I know." Maria leaned her head back on the couch.

The musty smell of old fabric enveloped her. She was so glad she wasn't allergic to dust. "I just feel like we should be doing something, and I don't know what to do."

"You think something bad's happened to him, don't you?" Isabel said.

"Don't you?" Maria turned slightly. "You're the one who keeps saying we should focus on him."

"Yeah." Liz leaned against the kitchen counter. "What does that mean, exactly?"

"I don't know." Isabel opened a drawer, then another, and another. "Doesn't he have garbage bags?"

"Michael?" Maria asked. "Are you kidding?"

"Then what does he do?"

"Uses paper bags under the sink," Maria said.

Isabel opened the sink cabinet and pulled out one of those bags, neatly folded, probably the only neatly folded item in the entire apartment. She shook it open and started to stuff pizza boxes inside.

"What does it mean?" Maria asked.

"What does what mean?" Isabel asked. The stench was growing. Obviously some of these pizza boxes had lived on the kitchen counter for a long time.

"That we should focus on him," Maria said.

Isabel sighed. She set aside one full bag and reached for another.

"Isabel." Liz caught her arm. "You had something in mind."

"Yeah," Isabel said, wrenching her arm away, "but it isn't working."

"What isn't working?" Maria asked.

Isabel washed her hands, then looked around for a

towel. When she didn't find one (where did she think she was, anyway?), she wiped her hands on her jeans.

"Remember when Michael's—granddaughter, or whatever you wanted to call her—was trapped in the woods?"

"Yeah?" Maria would never forget that. The days she'd spent with Michael at his real family's estate had made her understand him even more.

"I kept dreaming about her and getting flashes of her, remember?"

"I do," Liz said, nodding.

"And when Tess was trapped in the old power plant, I kept seeing her."

Maria remembered that. How pale Isabel had gotten at her birthday party, how bad those headaches were, and how lost she seemed.

Isabel's gaze met Maria's. "I'm not getting any of that from Michael."

Isabel's words were soft, but they sent a chill through Maria. "You can't be thinking that," Maria said.

"Thinking what?" Liz looked at both of them.

"He's not dead!" Maria said.

"But I should have a sense of him," Isabel said.

"Wait. Wait." Liz stood between them. "I thought Tess sent you the images of where she was trapped."

"She did, but—"

"And the others came to you in a dream, right?"

"Most of the time, although I always had the sense it was happening, that it was true."

"So what's the problem?" Maria asked. "Maybe you just can't sense Michael."

Isabel shook her head. "Michael and I have always

been really close. Brother and sister close. Almost as close as me and Max."

"I know that," Maria said and heard the defensiveness in her voice.

"So I should get a sense of him. I should know where he is and what's going on."

"It doesn't work like that," Liz said.

Isabel turned toward her. "He should let me know. He should send something to me."

"He doesn't have Tess's powers." Maria stood. She was beginning to understand what was going on. Isabel was as upset as she was, only she'd been hiding it under that cool exterior.

"But we're close. I should know."

Maria nodded. "So should I."

"You didn't know what happened to Max when they took him to the white room," Liz said.

"But I found him," Isabel said.

"With some dedicated dreaming." Liz took her arm and pulled her out of the kitchen. "You're even closer to Max than you are to Michael and you didn't know about him."

Maria felt a little shiver run through her. "Can you do the dream-walking with Michael?"

"I can try," Isabel said. "But you'd think I would have gotten something last night, if he was in trouble."

"Maybe he's not," Liz said. "Maybe he's off investigating that scam."

Isabel shook her head. "He would have let us know by now."

"Michael's not always considerate," Maria said, aware

that she had made the same argument Isabel was making just a little while ago.

Isabel threaded her fingers together. "I just have no sense of him at all. It really worries me."

"What about the dream-walking?" Liz asked again. She seemed to be the only calm one in the room.

"Yeah," Maria said. "It's worked before."

Isabel nodded. "Let's do it."

"Right here?" Maria asked.

"Yes," Isabel said. "I'd get a better sense of him then."

"Wait," Liz said. "If you get in trouble, neither Maria nor I can help you. We need Max here before you start."

"We can try it," Maria said. She wanted to get this going right now. The sooner they found Michael, the sooner she could rest.

"No," Liz said, her tone firm. "It's not safe."

"She's right," Isabel said. "We have to have either Max or Tess here. We don't know what Michael's dealing with. Sometimes the dream images are really powerful."

She shuddered. Maria wondered what she was remembering.

"And since we don't know, the best thing to do is to make sure someone can help me."

Maria sighed. "Okay. Well, they'll come here after they meet with that reporter."

"Which shouldn't take too long," Liz said.

"But what do we do while we wait?" Isabel asked.

All three of them looked at each other.

"I think I have garbage bags in the car," Maria said.

"Great," Isabel said. "You think he has a vacuum around here?"

All three of them looked at each other, and then, spontaneously, burst into laughter. Michael with a vacuum cleaner was too strange an image.

It was the very first laugh of the day. It felt good, but it also felt like a betrayal. Maria didn't want to enjoy herself when Michael could be in trouble.

She didn't want to do anything—except bring him home.

Nila set her purse down on the bed. She checked the phone for messages. She had none. Her cell phone hadn't rung either.

She pushed back one of the chairs near the window and sat down. Her laptop was still open on the table, the morning's newspaper spread on the other side. Between her and the window was a heating unit, and outside a view of the parking lot followed by lots of scrub.

Why would anyone stay in this place? Or better yet, why would anyone move here?

That was one of the many questions she'd wanted to ask Brody Davis, and she hadn't been able to. He had let her into the UFO Center, and he had shown her the back. He had a lot of equipment there, most of which she didn't get a good peek at.

Instead, he'd taken her to part of the UFO Center that had floor-to-ceiling pictures of the 1947 crash and a scale model replica of the supposed space ship hanging from the ceiling. It felt creepy sitting there, but Nila didn't let on. She didn't want Brody to know that he could unnerve her.

She had asked him a few perfunctory questions that he had answered while looking nervously over his shoulder.

Then she'd asked about his daughter Sydney, and he'd held his hand up to stop her.

"I told you," he said, "we're going to respect Sydney's privacy."

Nila had nodded. "I'm not going to use her name, just like I'd said before."

He didn't relax, but his gaze met hers for the first time. She had the very real sense that he was afraid of her. "Then what do you want to know?"

"What was her prognosis the night you had her air-lifted to Phoenix?"

"Critical," he said.

"What was wrong?"

"They told me she had an incurable form of childhood leukemia. I didn't think she'd see another Christmas." Like all the parents she'd talked with, he said this in a matter-of-fact manner. He hadn't come to terms with it, exactly, but it had been part of his life and nothing could change that.

"What happened in the hospital?"

"I don't know," he said. "I wasn't in the room."

Nila realized at that point that she'd have to take the interview slowly. "So what's her prognosis now?"

"She's cured."

"The disease is not in remission?"

"No," he said. "It's gone."

"When did that change?"

"You know when it did," he said.

"Tell me anyway."

"December twenty-fourth."

"What does Sydney say happened?"

"She says an angel healed her."

"What do you say?"

"I say I don't know."

Nila had a lot of questions prepared as follow-ups, and she knew some of them would offend Brody. Initially, when he'd said the bit about the angel, she had planned to say, *Do you think that for Sydney, angels are a way of explaining something she doesn't understand?* No matter how he answered that, she would have added, *Like aliens are for you?*

But after her meeting with Isabel Evans, Nila decided not to alienate Brody. She might need him for more deep background.

"So is she getting any further treatment?" Nila asked.

"No," Brody said. "She's not sick anymore."

"Do you think I could talk with her?"

"No," Brody said. He stood. "This interview is over."

"I do have a few more questions," Nila had said.

"No," and with that, Brody walked away.

Nila hadn't been too phased. She'd had interviews like that before. The problem was that it didn't leave her in a good position to request a follow-up—and she might need one.

Also, she hadn't been planning on staying in Roswell longer than she had to.

She sighed and tapped the space bar on her laptop, making the dark screen light. Her notes were still open, which was fine. She had nothing to hide. But in the future, she'd be better off shutting down her laptop and putting it away whenever she left the hotel room.

A knock on the door startled her. She hadn't given her room number to anyone. And whenever hotel staff knocked, they were supposed to identify themselves as they knocked.

She went to the door and peered through the peephole. Max stood outside her room. A short blonde whose face Nila couldn't see stood beside him.

How did they find her? Had the front desk given out her room number? If so, she'd have a talk with them before she checked out. They probably didn't get many businesswomen traveling alone through this part of New Mexico, but such practices could lead to lawsuits if the wrong people got wind of the room number.

She took a deep breath, steeling herself for the meeting and the attitude she'd have to show to get her information. Then she pulled the door open.

"Apparently you spoke to your sister," Nila said as she stepped aside.

"Yes." Max walked into the room, his entire body obviously tense. He seemed like he was on high alert.

The girl with him was Tess. As she came inside, she gave Nila a look of pure distaste.

Nila shut the door. "I don't know if Isabel told you who I am. I'm—"

"She showed me your card." Max turned around. He was taller than she was and that, in combination with those eyes, made him seem very strong.

Nila felt uneasy for the first time since she had come to Roswell.

"Well, then," she said, "have a seat. We have much to discuss."

"We'll stand." Max's voice had that flat edge of authority to it. Tess stood beside him, the way a wife would stand beside her more famous spouse. "What did you want to say to me?"

"It'll take a moment, Max," Nila said, deliberately using his first name. "You and Tess would be more comfortable if you sat."

"We're fine." Tess used the same clipped tone that Max had. If Nila hadn't read about Max and Liz in the guidance counselor's notes, she would have thought that Max and Tess were a couple of long-standing.

"All right." Nila walked past them. When her back was to them, she winced.

Already she had lost control of this interview. She closed her laptop and leaned against the heating unit. Fortunately it was off. Her only other choice was to sit, and that would put her at even more of a disadvantage.

"Have you found your friend yet?" she asked.

Max's eyes widened slightly. She had surprised him. He had been bracing himself for another question. "No."

"I'm sorry. I know you're all worried about him."

"Do you know anything about his disappearance?" Tess asked. She had taken a step forward.

Nila smiled. The girl was a firecracker, and a bit unpredictable. It was clear by Max's light touch to Tess's arm that he didn't approve of that question.

"No, I don't know anything about his disappearance," Nila said. "Although I do know where he went on December twenty-fourth."

Max let his hand drop from Tess's arm, but he didn't say anything. Isabel had prepared him well.

"He was with you, Max, in Phoenix. He stood guard

while you disappeared into the Pediatric Oncology ward and did whatever it was you did to those children."

Max stared at her. His gaze made her uncomfortable.

"You were filmed," she said. "I have your face and your friend Michael's on security video."

"How do you know what Michael looks like?" Tess asked. "Have you seen him?"

The implication was clear. The girl was accusing her of lying about the disappearance.

"I do a lot of research when I'm working on a story," Nila said. "I saw a picture of Michael in the local newspaper. Seems he got himself legal permission to handle his own affairs even though he's underage. Sounds like your friend Michael has had a hard life."

Max didn't take the bait. She wanted him to ask about Michael. Instead, Max asked, "What story are you researching?"

"I would have thought Isabel told you," Nila said. "You did get to my room awfully fast."

"Isabel said you made a threat."

"And it's your job to defend the world against threats?" Nila asked, intrigued.

"Against me," Max said.

"Ah, and that upsets you."

"What upsets me," he said slowly and with great emphasis, "is that someone blocked my sister in our driveway, and then threatened her. The content of the threat doesn't matter. The action does. If you have a problem with me, you come to me."

How old was this kid? He didn't say that the way a

teenager would, all bravado and machismo. He said it flatly, the way a forty-year-old man with great power would. The way someone would if he knew he could squash his opponent like a bug, but really preferred not to.

"All right," Nila said, and pushed herself off the heater. "Let me take this step by step. It's a federal offense to sell illegal drugs."

"What?" Tess asked. Max caught her arm again and pulled her close, almost as if he were holding her back.

"The offense is compounded when any transaction to deal with those drugs happens through the mail. If cash, for example, is sent from New Mexico to Arizona, then the offense is compounded a third time because the criminals have now crossed state lines. Are you with me, Max?"

Max shook his head. "I have no idea what you're talking about."

"The serum," she said. "The stuff you used to heal the kids. Did you know someone is selling it over the Internet?"

Max looked stunned. "What serum?"

Nila had expected him to deny knowing of the Internet sales, but she hadn't expected him to deny the serum. He didn't seem to be scamming her, although she knew some people were really good at covering how they felt and what they thought.

Instead of giving him a direct answer, she grabbed her laptop and opened one of her files. She swung the machine so that the screen faced Max and Tess.

Tess's eyes grew wide as she read.

Max's face got pale.

Nila knew what they were reading almost by heart. The web site started out with a banner ad for the serum, then had a lot of information for sick children and their parents. The Christmas Miracle was halfway down the page, cited as an example of the way that the researchers had tried to show the world how their serum worked— and why they should not be denied legal sales in the United States.

"Where did this come from?" Max asked.

"I was hoping you could tell me." Nila set the laptop down. Tess went toward it, sat in a chair, and continued reading. Nila kept an eye on her—she didn't want Tess to get into the other files.

"I know nothing about this," Max said.

"Yet you know what happened in that hospital," Nila said.

Max was silent.

She recognized the silence. It was, in its own way, a victory. If he didn't know, he would deny in the exact same way he had when she mentioned the serum.

The fact that he hadn't denied was intriguing. She would wager he was trying not to lie to her. Max had integrity—or he thought he did. Or he was trying to convince her that he did. He certainly was smart enough.

Maybe he had been surprised by the sale of the serum. Maybe he would go back to the Crashdown or that nice house of his family's and call the researchers, asking them for a cut. As composed as this kid was, Nila wouldn't put anything past him.

"I've come close to these guys twice," she said, deciding to trade information for trust. It was a risk. If Max was involved with the scam artists, they would learn she was on their trail. Of course, it wasn't much of a risk since they probably knew it anyway—after her meeting with Isabel.

Tess was still reading the screen. The file was still the one on the serum.

"I found their post office box, not that that was hard—all I had to do was send them a sob story about a sick child. I saw the man who picked up the mail. He was the suspicious sort, though, so I had to tail him from some distance. I lost him."

Max was staring at her so intently that she felt uncomfortable. To hide the feeling, she returned to her perch on the heating unit.

"So I went back to the post office a few days later and waited in my car. Sure enough, he showed up again, and left carrying packages. I assumed those packages contained the cash. I followed him again, and this time I was able to stay with him."

Max moved just slightly. She took that for interest.

Tess had clicked on a new file. As the file opened, Nila grabbed the laptop and closed the lid.

"Nope," she said to Tess. "The rest of the stuff on this machine is private."

"Sorry," Tess said in a tone that said she wasn't sorry at all. She pushed her chair back and rested in it, watching Nila through her thick eyelashes.

"Anyway," Nila said, "I tracked him to a place just outside of Florence Junction. He turned off on a dirt road that looked like it didn't get a lot of use. I couldn't follow him down that, so I didn't even try. But I'll figure out a way to get there. It won't be hard."

Max blinked, glanced at Tess, who gave him a small, elegant shrug. Nila had no idea what they were communicating about—telling her that they knew about this? Working with her? Concern? She supposed she'd find out soon enough.

"These guys are good," Nila said. "The police haven't gotten the serum, mostly because they haven't gotten any complaints about it. They can't move on these guys until they know for sure that they aren't selling sugar water through the mail."

"That would be fraud," Tess said.

"Fraud and drug trafficking are two different things," Nila said.

Tess leaned back farther, not taking her gaze from Nila. "You could order the stuff. You have the address."

"But not the fifteen thousand," Nila said. "Although I have considered it."

"But?" Max asked.

Nila smiled. "That's where you come in."

"I don't understand," Max said.

"I think you do," she said.

"Well, I don't." Tess stood up and put her hands into her back pockets. "Explain it to me."

Nila didn't look at her. Her concentration was on the smart, powerful and young Max Evans. "You're involved in this. The police have studied that hospital security video a hundred times. They have no idea who you are, but I do."

Max's gaze narrowed. Tess walked to his side. Nila felt a prickle of unease. She didn't let it show.

"I'll give you to them, unless you help me," she said.

"Help you how?" Max asked.

"I know the serum sold on that site is a scam. I want proof. I want the men who are conducting it. If you help me get them, I'll make sure no one ever knows you were involved."

"Until your articles come out," Tess said.

Nila shook her head. "Not even then."

"Why should we trust you?" Tess asked.

Max put his hand on her shoulder. Tess looked up at him, then she frowned. Apparently she didn't like what she saw in his eyes.

"I'll do it," he said.

"Max," Tess said, her tone a warning.

"Good," Nila said.

"Will you be here later tonight?" Max asked.

"Yes," Nila said.

"I'll talk to you then."

With that, he took Tess by the arm and led her from the room. She glanced over her shoulder once, and another shiver ran through Nila. What was it about that girl that made Nila feel she could kill with a single look?

The door closed behind them, and Nila let out a small breath. Then she cursed. She hurried to the door, but Max and Tess were already gone.

She should have gotten his help while he was here. She should have taken it that extra step, and she hadn't.

From the moment he entered the room, Max had controlled the meeting. Nila had been around charisma before, but she had never fallen victim to it.

Until now.

It would be just her luck that he would warn the scam artists.

Or try to take them on himself.

She cursed again. Now it was her turn to trust him—and she didn't like the feeling. She didn't like it at all.

10

March 24—Florence Junction, Arizona

Jerry entered the dining room, still wiping his hands with the hand towel. Whoever had first called money filthy lucre was right. His hands had an oily feel when he and Dane had finished counting.

Money always felt odd to Jerry—cash in particular, as if just by touching it, he was touching all the hands the money had passed through. It reminded him how transient the stuff was. Cash could be spent without a trace, at least as far as the cops were concerned, but the trace was there. Fingerprints, grease, cooking oil, even blood. If a substance was on someone's fingers when they touched a bill, the substance was on the paper.

And then it got transferred to Jerry's hands.

He shivered and wiped his hands again. He'd already washed them three times. The first time Dane had seen him do that, Dane had laughed.

"Who're you, Judas? Can't get the bloody feel of those thirty pieces of silver off your hands?"

The comment was more accurate than Jerry would have liked. Part of this scam made him feel really guilty. The part that had to do with the kids.

Sure, the parents were victims of their own desperation, but the kids were the real victims here—of the malfunctioning of their own bodies, of a medical system that didn't find answers quickly enough, of parents who believed in miracles.

Jerry wouldn't have been able to handle this scam year after year. The three months he and Dane had been doing it already seemed too long.

In the past, Jerry's scams had all been geared toward suckers. He firmly believed the P. T. Barnum maxim that there was one born every minute—and like Barnum, he planned to take advantage of all of those brain-dead folks.

When Jerry had seen the so-called Christmas Miracle on TV, he knew he had something he could use. And when no one came forward to claim credit, he was positive he could use it. He didn't think of the implications for the kids until later, until the first package of filthy lucre had come through the door.

By then it was too late.

He trusted Dane, he really did, but he trusted Dane to be consistent. And the one thing he knew Dane hated most in the world was to be disappointed by his friends.

Jerry had set up a scam that worked. They had actual money in their hands, with the promise of more. It was a simple plan, one that took almost no effort on their part.

If Jerry backed out, Dane would have seen that as a

disappointment, a personal affront, committed by a friend. The last time one of Dane's friends had disappointed him, the friend had received a homemade knife in the belly—and hadn't lived.

Jerry had to see this scam through, for his own sake. Thank heavens it was nearly done.

He set the towel on the dining room table and sat down by the computer. The little envelope icon on the bar was blinking. He had mail.

The kitchen door opened, and Dane came out. He was carrying a Styrofoam cooler.

"I swear," he said with a grin. "This is the best stuff I've ever made. It even tastes good. And I bet there's enough alcohol in here from the various cough syrups to give the kids a good buzz before they go to sleep."

"They don't need a buzz, Dane," Jerry said. He wished Dane would stop tampering with the stuff. They had a product that worked. Jerry was secretly afraid that some of those cough medications wouldn't go together—or something new that Dane put into the mixture would cause some kind of allergic reaction in one of those already-sick kids.

So far it hadn't happened. Or at least, if it had, no one had blamed the medication. They had blamed whatever disease had killed the kid.

"The secret is Karo syrup," Dane said. "It's thicker and sweeter now. The kids will love it."

"They're not supposed to love it," Jerry said, clicking on his mail program. "Medicine is supposed to be nasty."

Dane rested the ice chest on the edge of the dining room table. "What got up your butt?"

The feel of the money against his hands, money made from sick kids. Jerry had to bury those thoughts, just like he had been doing.

At least, he told parents to continue getting regular medical care for their kids. The serum wouldn't make the kids well, but it wouldn't hurt them either—so far as he knew.

He was really over his head in this one. Best scam he'd ever come up with and he didn't have the balls for it. Hell, he didn't even have the balls to admit that to his partner.

"Jerry?" Dane asked.

"Nothing," Jerry said. "Nothing's up. I'm just tired, is all, and ready to get out of this hellhole."

"Yeah, me too. But it won't take too long and we'll be saying *"Adios, amigos."*

Not a moment too soon. Jerry downloaded his mail. While he was doing that, he opened the letters that he'd left unread in the box.

"So, we ready?" Dane asked.

"Let me check." Jerry scanned the return addresses until he saw the one he was looking for. "Yep. We got an okay from our latest."

"Good," Dane said. "The GasMart, I hope."

The GasMart, at the junction of Interstate 10 and state highway 80, was Dane's favorite drop spot because there was the Pie 'N' Stuff diner across the street. Dane had a thing going with one of the waitresses, and he didn't think Jerry knew about it.

But Jerry kept his eye on Dane. That was the problem with having partners. They always threw a monkey wrench into the works—and never in the way that Jerry expected. So he'd learned over the years to be vigilant. Sometimes he could stop a problem before it started.

"Yes," he said. "The GasMart."

"Excellent!" Dane said, grinning.

Jerry did not grin back. "You better get going. I want you there at least three hours ahead, making sure there are no cops."

"You got it," Dane said, taking the small cooler and heading for the door, whistling an old Jerry Reed tune.

"Hey, Dane," Jerry said.

"Yeah?" Dane turned slightly.

"Do the waitress after the drop, okay?"

Dane grinned. "We ain't done nothing yet, Jer."

"I just don't want you to forget to watch your back."

Dane's grin faded. "I've never forgotten that, Jer. In fact, it's something I never forget."

So it was out in the open. The lack of trust between them. Jerry could comment on Dane's actions, on his own discomfort, but he didn't think there was a point.

Not yet.

"I'm glad you don't forget it," Jerry said. "Good luck with this one."

"You think I'll need it?" Dane asked.

"I think the more we do this, the more luck we need," Jerry said. "I'm glad we're almost at our target."

Dane shifted the ice chest. "Me, too, partner. Me, too."

11

March 24—Scottsdale, Arizona

Michael was getting uncomfortable. His right foot was falling asleep. He was beginning to think his plan—waiting until Chad Newcomb (the guy finally introduced himself) was ready to spill—wasn't going to work.

Michael was rethinking the whole thing. Only he wasn't sure how he'd get out of this weird pink room, not without revealing himself and his powers.

The early afternoon light was coming in both windows now. The room had changed from Pepto-Bismol pink to Barbie pink. It felt like Michael was sitting in one of the rooms of the Barbie Dream House that Isabel used to have.

The Dream House he had methodically melted one afternoon after being forced to move a Ken doll from the door to the Corvette and back again too many times.

He'd been banned from the Evans's house for a week by Isabel. And she and Max had never told on him, not once, for all the things he did. Melting the Barbie Dream House was by far the most minor.

Sometimes he wondered how he ever lived with himself in those days.

Then he glanced at little Katie. She hadn't moved from the bed. Once she'd stirred and sighed—a moan, really—and Chad had been at her side in a heartbeat. The guy was completely dedicated to her, which made this even harder.

Something had to happen, but Michael didn't know what that something was.

Newcomb was sitting at the tiny table, only he didn't go near the chairs. He sat cross-legged on the floor, facing Katie, so that he could keep an eye on her while he worked on his computer. He'd been downloading e-mail: Michael had recognized the odd digital tones of a modem connecting, and then the beeps and blips of an e-mail program like the ones he'd used at school.

Newcomb really hadn't been paying a lot of attention to him. Apparently Newcomb thought Michael was tied up pretty good. Instead, Newcomb was staring fixedly at the computer screen, as if he saw something he didn't like.

Then he muttered something under his breath and got up, heading out of the room with great determination.

Michael waited until Newcomb was gone, then glanced at Katie. She was still asleep. He doubted she even knew that he was in the room. She hadn't opened her eyes at all, and really looked at him, since he arrived.

He widened the ropes holding his hands, but didn't untie the knot. There was no way he could retie it behind him.

Newcomb's voice came from the front room, frantic. Michael caught a few words every other sentence or so.

"...watch her for a few hours..."

Michael held out his free hand and spun the laptop toward him. The screen was still lit. It hadn't gone to sleep yet.

"...pay you as much as you want..."

The e-mail letter was still open. Michael didn't recognize the return address.

"...need someone I trust to baby-sit for just a few..."

He scanned the message quickly.

"...no. I need to know the person. It's Katie's life..."

The message was a series of directions for the serum drop. Michael caught his breath.

"...please. You're my last hope. I don't know what I'm..."

They wanted Newcomb to drive to some GasMart fifty miles east of Tucson, at the junction of Interstate 10 and state highway 80. Michael knew where that was.

"...I don't want her back in that hospital. They're not helping..."

He'd been to the GasMart a dozen times. It was on the freeway between Roswell and Phoenix, almost to the New Mexico border. From there, highway 80 went south to the Old West town of Tombstone, and then on to the Mexican border.

"...my last hope. Please, Mary, you've sat with her before..."

Michael glanced at the computer's clock. The meeting was scheduled for four hours from now and the drive took three. Newcomb had better get off the phone and get moving if he wanted to make that meeting.

"...I know she wasn't that sick then, but..."

Michael memorized the directions, then turned the computer around to its original position.

"...no! please! I don't know who else to call—" Newcomb's voice broke off. Michael heard a receiver get slammed down.

Michael reached behind him and slipped his hands into the ropes. He made the ropes tighten, but not as bad as before.

His right foot was asleep now. He should have loosened those bonds while Newcomb was out of the room, but he was concentrating on the computer instead.

Newcomb came back inside just as Michael finished with the ropes. He glanced at Michael, then at Katie.

"I caught part of the conversation," Michael said. "What's happening?"

"I have to meet your friends."

"The serum guys?"

"Yeah," Newcomb said.

"What about Katie?"

"She's coming with me."

"Man, she's really sick. Why don't you just take her back to the hospital?"

The look Newcomb gave him was so full of despair that Michael felt it himself. "This is our last hope," he said.

"What about me? You gonna leave me here?"

Newcomb studied him for a minute, as if he hadn't given Michael any thought at all. "What if they recognize you from the hospital?"

"They won't," Michael said. He had to go along on this

trip. He had to find these idiots and stop this scam before others got hurt.

"Will you behave?"

"Scout's honor," Michael said, even though he had never been a scout.

"If something happens to Katie because of you—"

"It won't," Michael said, resisting the urge to say that if anyone hurt Katie, it would be Newcomb. Taking her out of here was as stupid as taking her out of the hospital in the first place. "Where're we going?"

"You don't need to know," Newcomb said.

"It would help if I did," Michael said.

"Yeah," Newcomb said. "It would help you."

Michael sighed and leaned back. There was no arguing with this guy. The best thing about taking Katie—in fact, the only good thing—was that the GasMart was hours closer to Max. If Michael got the chance to get to a phone, he might be able to get Max to meet him there.

If he got to a phone, which wasn't likely, looking at Newcomb's face.

"I'm going to get the car ready," Newcomb said. "We don't have a lot of time."

"Okay," Michael said.

"If you're going to give me trouble, I'll have to drug you and put you in the trunk."

Michael felt a surge of panic. He wasn't going to let that happen. He wasn't going to be unconscious again, even if preventing it made him reveal his powers.

"I already promised I'll be good," Michael said, sounding like a little kid.

Newcomb nodded. He gave Katie one last look, and then grabbed some blankets from her closet.

Michael watched him go, calculating how much time he had. He listened to Newcomb's steps fade away. A door opened in the distance, and then he heard nothing.

This would be his only chance.

Michael scanned the room for the phone. There wasn't one. He should have realized that. He had heard the phone ring, but not in here.

But the computer had a modem line and he'd seen a phone icon.

In the distance, footsteps sounded. Michael tried to look relaxed. Newcomb came back into the room, grabbed a couple of medicine vials and a stuffed animal, and left again.

The sound of his footsteps seemed to go in the same direction as they had before.

Michael's mouth was dry. He unhooked his right hand as he had done before and, using his weight, moved the chair three steps sideways. He clicked on the phone icon, got the phone up, and was relieved to see that it had been programmed.

He would only have one phone call, and he wasn't sure who to call. Max wouldn't be home during the day. There was no telling where anyone was.

Michael had only a half second to consider, and then he dialed, praying he'd get an answer.

12

March 24—Roswell, New Mexico

Isabel tucked a strand of hair behind her ear. She wished she had worn her hair pulled back in a ponytail like she often did. She was constantly trying to keep it from getting into the unidentifiable goo that covered Michael's countertops.

Hadn't anyone taught him to wipe up his messes? She was convinced there were soda stains that dated from the day he first moved in. It was going to take some really incredible cleanser to get the sticky stuff off without taking off the countertop, too.

"What is this?" Liz asked, holding a slimy green bag by its ragged edge.

"Don't go there," Maria said. The work of cleaning the kitchen seemed to agree with her. She hadn't snapped at anyone in at least ten minutes.

Not that Isabel blamed her. She felt like snapping at people, too.

There was a knock on the door and all three of them stopped. Maria had a look of stunned surprise on her face before she realized that it couldn't be Michael at the door. He wouldn't knock on the door to his own place.

Liz glanced at Isabel.

"Who is it?" she yelled.

"Max and Tess."

Maria ran to the door. The sooner they came in, the quicker they could try to reach Michael. They'd all been frustrated by the wait—and the incredible mess in this place.

At least, Isabel had.

Maria pulled the door open. Max and Tess came inside. Tess's mouth was a thin line. She didn't look happy. Isabel couldn't read Max. That was happening more and more. It was as if a part of him had grown a shield, one that she couldn't reach through.

"What happened?" she asked, setting down the current pizza box.

"Max wants to help that reporter." Tess sounded as unhappy as she looked.

"Max?" Isabel asked.

Max gave her a miserable look. "She knows we were at the hospital, Isabel. She has a security tape with me and Michael on it. She knows we're connected somehow and she's threatening to give us up to the police."

"Unless you do what?" Isabel held her hands up. She'd have to wash them before she left the kitchen. Her fingers felt slimy.

"Help her find these people running the drug ring."

"But I thought she believes you're involved," Isabel said.

"She does," Tess said.

Isabel could tell she wasn't just unhappy. She was furious.

"She thinks Max can lead her directly to them," Tess said, "for this article she's writing."

"You don't trust her," Liz said, stating the obvious as she often did.

"Nasedo would have killed her," Tess said.

Maria gave her an incredulous look. "Is that what you want to do?"

"What I want to do and what I can do are two different things," Tess said. "But she's a threat."

Isabel turned on the faucet and ran her hands under the hot water. At least Michael had soap.

"And you think Max going with her is the wrong idea?"

"I know it," Tess said.

"I don't think we have a choice," Max said.

"I don't think you want us to have a choice," Tess said. "You want to go after those people."

Isabel wiped her hands on a paper towel. She looked across the counter into the living room. Max was watching her. Now she could read him—probably because he wanted her to.

"They're making money off children," Isabel said. "I don't think Max can stomach that."

"It's more than that," he said. "They're scamming people who have almost no hope. When I—"

He shook his head and turned away.

"When you what?" Liz asked.

He took a deep breath. He clearly didn't want to talk about this and was probably upset that he had mentioned it.

"Max?" Maria asked.

He sighed. "When I healed those children, I saw everything. Their births—the parents were so happy. They thought they saw the future, you know? And when the kids learned to walk, and how much love there was around them. That's what these creeps are preying on. They're preying on dying dreams and too much love."

"And hopelessness," Liz said.

"Exactly." Max turned to her. Tess's look of disapproval grew.

"But there's more to it than that." Isabel threw the paper towel into the open garbage sack. "They couldn't run this scam if Max hadn't saved all those lives."

Max shoved his hands into his pockets and walked toward the window, his back to all of them. That was what bothered him the most, and Isabel knew it.

Michael had a saying—a saying she hated, but she knew Max was thinking about it: No good deed goes unpunished. This was Max's punishment for helping those kids.

"They could be killing kids with their serum. They may be bankrupting families." Max bowed his head. "I've got to do something."

"But you don't have to risk your life to do it," Tess said.

"Yes," Max said. "I do."

No one spoke for a moment. Then Maria said, "What about Michael?"

"I don't think she knows where he is," Tess said.

"He might have gone after them, too," Max said. "We just don't know until we figure out something."

Maria inclined her head toward Isabel. This, apparently, was her cue.

"I could try to dream-walk," she said.

Max turned. "Michael would have to be asleep for that to work," he said.

"You were floating in and out of consciousness," Isabel said. "It worked then."

Max nodded. "You think maybe this will work?"

"Yeah," Isabel said. What she didn't say, what she knew Max understood, was that Michael had to be drugged, asleep, or in serious trouble for this to work.

"Why didn't you try it already?" Tess asked.

"We waited for you guys," Liz said. "We wanted help here if something happened to Isabel."

Tess's wide-eyed gaze met Isabel's. Finally, understanding on her part, too. This might not be about a serum or a reporter. It could be Skins or others from their home planet. Or a new threat none of them had heard of.

"How do you plan to do this?" Max asked.

"I thought I'd focus on Michael," Isabel said. "I'd just lie on the couch and see if I could doze off. If I do, then if he's asleep, it might work."

Max nodded. "I told the reporter I'd be back tonight, so we have some time."

"All right," Isabel said. "Let's give it a shot."

She walked over to the couch and lay down, carefully avoiding the raised spring. The couch had almost no support, but the cushions were soft.

"You actually think you can sleep on that thing?" Maria asked.

"Isabel can fall asleep anywhere," Max said.

Isabel closed her eyes. She was tired. All she had to do was relax, and if she relaxed, then she'd fall asleep....

Maria hovered near the couch. How anyone could sleep on that thing was beyond her. Anyone except Michael, that is. Michael could fall asleep on the floor, in a car, in class—anywhere, just like Isabel.

Maybe it was an alien trait.

Isabel's breathing had evened out. She was falling asleep. Liz looked at Maria and shrugged. Apparently she had no idea what to do.

Neither did Maria. They didn't dare make noise—it might wake Isabel—and they couldn't talk.

Maybe this was a bad idea, after all. Maria needed to keep busy. She was a lot happier when they were cleaning this place than she was just standing around.

Then a phone rang.

The entire group looked at each other—except Isabel, who was still sleeping.

The phone rang again, and four people jumped into action. Max went for Michael's phone and Tess reached into her purse. Liz grabbed her purse off the coffee table, and Maria searched for hers. Where did she leave it?

Max picked up Michael's phone, Tess answered her cell, and so did Liz, but the ringing continued.

Maria finally saw her purse under a chair near the door. She grabbed the purse, pulled out her phone, and answered it.

"Jeez, the one time I need you to answer the phone fast." It was Michael. Her heart leapt.

"Michael! Where are you?"

Everything stopped as everyone looked at her. Isabel was sitting up, rubbing the sleep from her eyes.

"Listen, Maria, I don't have a lot of time. If I stop talking, you stop too, okay? It's real important."

"Why? What's going on?"

"Just agree, okay?"

"Okay." Maria looked at everyone and shrugged. "Are you all right?"

"I'm fine, but I don't have time to chat. Just listen. No, wait. Be quiet for a minute, okay?"

"Okay, but—"

"No buts. Just shut up."

She did. No one in Michael's living room moved. Neither did she.

There was a clink on the phone and then an odd shuffling sound as if someone moved a chair. She heard Michael curse softly, and then nothing for a moment.

"What is it?" Max asked.

Maria put a finger to her lips. Max nodded.

An unfamiliar man's voice crooned in the background, followed by the muffled voice of a sleeping child.

"It'll be all right," the man said. "It's just for a little while."

There was rustling, followed by a sharp moan.

Maria held her breath.

"I'll be back for you," the man said. "No funny stuff."

"No funny stuff," Michael repeated.

Maria's heart started to pound.

What's going on? Liz mouthed.

I don't know, Maria mouthed back.

Isabel was biting her lower lip. Tess was frowning. Max had come closer, as if just being near the phone gave him some answers.

Then Maria heard that weird shuffling noise again, and an odd beep that sounded like it came from a computer.

"Okay," Michael said. "Now just listen. I'm fine, but I need you guys to meet me at the GasMart at the junction of Interstate 10 and Arizona state highway 80. That's about fifty miles east of Tucson. Got that?"

"Yeah," Maria said. "What's going on?"

"Repeat it back to me." He sounded distracted.

"The GasMart at the junction of 10 and 80 fifty miles east of Tucson." Maria pointed to Liz as she said that. Liz scrambled for some paper and wrote it down. "Are you there now?"

"No, but I will be in a few hours. If I'm not there right away, wait for me, okay?"

"Okay," Maria said. "Who was that guy?"

"Gotta run," Michael said, and the connection ended.

"Michael! Michael!" Maria looked at the phone in exasperation. "He hung up."

"What's going on?" Isabel said.

"I have no idea. I heard a guy and a kid in the background and someone moaned. Michael was being all secretive."

"What's this about meeting him?" Max asked.

Maria shrugged. "Did you get it, Liz?"

"Interstate 80 and 10, fifty miles east of Tucson," she said, reading off the note.

"He wants us to meet him there in a few hours," Maria said.

"He can't mean Interstate 80," Isabel said. "That's clear up north."

"Arizona 80," Maria said, glaring at Liz. "And Interstate 10. At the junction. We're supposed to go to a GasMart."

"Is he all right?" Max asked.

"He said he was."

"What's he doing?" Isabel asked.

"He didn't say. He was in a hurry."

"He's up to something," Isabel said.

"You said there was a kid?" Tess asked.

"And he's in Arizona." Max looked at Tess. Tess shook her head.

"What?" Liz asked.

"He's working on the serum thing, just like we thought," Max said. "And he's setting something up."

"He's doing it alone?" Isabel asked.

"Not alone," Maria said. "He just asked for us."

"It seems like a bit of a jump to think he's working on that." Liz was still clutching the paper. "I mean, we don't have a lot to go on."

"It's Michael," Max said. "You always have to factor that in."

"Well," Tess said, a little more cheerfully than Maria would have liked. "Looks like you can't go with that reporter, after all."

"Sure we can," Max said. "She mentioned Florence Junction. That's in Arizona, not more than an hour from that GasMart."

"You're suggesting we split up?" Isabel asked.

"I think he wanted you there, too," Maria said.

"Did he ask for me?" Max said.

"He said 'you guys.' I think that means everyone."

"But he didn't specify, right?" Max asked.

Maria sighed. "No, he didn't. But I knew what he meant."

"Well, here's what we do. Tess and I will go with the reporter. If it looks like a dead end, we'll meet you at the GasMart. Bring your phones so we can stay in touch."

"I don't like this," Liz said. "We need you guys. Michael might need you."

"Yeah," Maria said. "Sometimes he doesn't know when he's in over his head."

"Tell you what," Max said. "Get Sheriff Valenti to go with you. And Alex. He has a good head on his shoulders."

"And Kyle," Tess said.

Max shook his head. "Let's station Kyle at the Crashdown. If Michael can't reach any of us, he'll call there. Kyle should be able to reach us somehow. He's pretty resourceful."

That last sounded begrudging from Max. He still hadn't gotten over the whole Liz/Kyle thing that led to the breakup. But he blamed Kyle more than Liz.

"I think you should come with us," Maria said. "I don't like this reporter idea."

"Neither do I," said Tess.

"Me, either," Isabel said.

"I think it's a sensible plan," Liz said.

Max smiled at her.

"Why would you think that?" Tess said. "What if Michael's hurt? Then what?"

"He said he was fine." Liz was looking at Max. "But

now we know he's not in serious trouble, or he would have said so. We can afford to have Max and Tess go after the scam guys."

"And you, Liz," Max said. "I'd like to have you with us."

"Why?" Tess asked.

Maria resisted the urge to roll her eyes.

"Liz seemed to have a connection with her at the restaurant. We might be able to use that to get information from her," Max said.

Maria didn't like it. "I'm not sure Michael is all right," she said.

"Why not?" Max asked.

"The guy on the phone told Michael no funny stuff," Maria said.

Everyone looked at her.

"Did Michael sound worried about that?" Max asked.

Maria reluctantly shook her head.

"Then we won't worry about it, either."

"Max," Isabel said. "I think it's irresponsible to go with the reporter—"

"No, Isabel," Max said. "If you think about it, you know I'm right. These guys are putting a lot of children's lives in jeopardy. Tess and I can stop them, and we will."

Maria sighed. Max was right. She hated it when he was right. "I hope you can do it fast."

"So do I," Max said. "Believe me, so do I."

13

March 24—Tucson, Arizona

Chad was full of doubts. His stomach was twisted in so many knots that he was nauseous, and his shoulders ached from the tension. Turning the steering wheel into sharp corners actually pulled muscles in his back.

He had a kid tied up in his front seat, and in the back, his critically ill daughter in her car seat.

The road stretched out before him, flat against the desert scrub. It seemed to stretch forever.

He knew Tucson was just ahead because the signs told him so, but like most things in the desert, the city seemed very far away.

Katie's breathing had changed in the last half hour. Chad was more familiar with the sound of Katie's breathing than he was with his own. When she had been a newborn, all red and wrinkled, he used to stand over her crib and watch her tiny chest rise and fall.

Sometimes he'd fall asleep in her room, lulled by the

sound of that even breath, in and out, in and out, as soothing as any sound he'd ever heard. Before Katie was born, Chad used to think the most precious, soothing sound he'd ever heard was Maggie's heartbeat, steady and even, as they cuddled together in their own bed.

When Katie came into the world, both he and Maggie listened to all the sounds she made, thinking there was nothing else like it on Earth.

Sometimes he regretted those last years, putting Katie first, because he didn't realize that he was going to lose his wife.

And now he was going to lose his daughter. He was chasing after scams and ghosts and fever dreams, jeopardizing his daughter's very life.

There weren't many other cars on the road, for which he was thankful. He had tied the boy tightly, but he still feared that someone would drive by and see the kid's hands tied in his lap.

To his credit, the boy didn't move much or say much. He seemed to be concentrating on the road ahead, although once or twice he glanced back at Katie, as if he were checking on her, too.

Her breathing had gotten even more raspy. Perhaps it was the desert air, being filtered through the car's air conditioner. Maggie believed that Katie had mild allergies to something that grew in the desert, because she used to sneeze so after hard rains. When the desert bloomed, Katie sneezed.

Chad had been so focused on his daughter that he hadn't noticed the rainstorm earlier in the week. He had probably been inside when it happened. The desert was in bloom, and it was beautiful.

Maggie used to love the desert in full flower.

Katie coughed and wheezed.

The boy glanced over his shoulder, an alarmed expression on his face.

Then Katie hacked and choked.

Chad started to pull over.

"No!" the boy yelled. He was out of his bonds and throwing himself into the backseat. "Keep going. She needs to get to a hospital."

He finished crawling over the seat and picked her out of the car seat, adjusting her position so that she could get more air.

Chad looked at them, the boy he'd kidnapped and his frail daughter, and watched the boy try to save her life. He stepped on the accelerator and sped down the highway.

He knew where the hospital was in Tucson. It was only a few miles from here. Normally, he'd think that was nothing. But a few miles was probably a few too many.

Katie's face was turning blue.

"Come on, kid, come on," Michael was muttering. "Breathe."

She was so small. He could feel her ribs and the knobs of her spine through her tiny shirt. She was burning up, and something was caught in her throat.

Her eyes were rolled in the back of her head, but he was afraid to do the Heimlich maneuver, afraid he'd make things worse by snapping her fragile bones.

If only Max were here. Max would be able to save her. But Max was still in New Mexico, on his way to the GasMart fifty miles east of here. Nowhere near close enough.

He could feel the car accelerating. Rocks, buildings and brush whizzed past the window, and so did the occasional car. Michael didn't think he'd ever been in a car that had gone this fast.

Newcomb was passing on the right, sometimes kicking up dust as he hit the shoulder. Michael prayed that Newcomb knew what he was doing—the road dropped off past the shoulder in some of these areas—and Newcomb might flip the car.

"Breathe, Katie," Michael said and patted her back gently. She was coughing now. He remembered hearing that that was a good sign. Coughing meant someone wasn't choking to death.

But her skin was still that sickly blue color and she was so hot. He'd never touched a human body that was so very hot.

Was she going to die in his arms? He wasn't sure he could take it. And he wasn't sure what he'd do to Newcomb if she did.

Of all the fool things, bringing a child who was this ill on a long road trip. Michael had asked about it once when they got into the car, and Newcomb had made up some lame excuse about not being able to find anyone to stay with her.

Then Michael had suggested taking her to the hospital in Phoenix and Newcomb had reacted as if Michael had suggested leaving her on the side of the road.

The man, in his fear and panic, was going to kill his own daughter.

"How close are we to that hospital?" Michael asked as Newcomb sped up the off ramp. If Newcomb didn't get her to an emergency room now, Michael was going to take over.

It was a risk he was willing to take.

Katie, in spite of the fact she was burning up, was shivering. Michael wrapped a blanket around her and continued to hold her close.

"The hospital?" he asked again. He knew he sounded panicked, but he didn't care. She needed help.

"Almost there," Newcomb said, swinging the car hard around a corner. "Is she all right?"

"No, she's not all right," Michael said. He wanted to say more. He wanted to say that she was dying, but he didn't know how much she could hear. "Just get her there, all right? And fast."

The car lurched into another corner and the buildings near the road flashed past. Michael had no idea how fast they were going.

But he was afraid it wasn't fast enough.

Chad followed the signs on the congested street. He'd broken every driving law he could think of. He'd used driveways as shortcuts, driven on sidewalks, and sped down turning lanes to get to this hospital.

It looked smaller than he remembered. They wouldn't be able to help Katie. The most famous children's ward in the Southwest hadn't been able to help Katie. There was no way this hospital—which didn't know Katie, wasn't familiar with her case, probably didn't even have the same equipment—would be able to help her.

She was going to die because he had made the wrong choices.

He skidded to a stop in front of the emergency room doors, pounding on the horn as hard as he could to get someone's attention. The doors slid open as he stopped and some nurses hurried out, along with a security guard.

Already Michael was getting out of the backseat, Katie in his arms. "Tell me where to put her," he said as he ran with her into the hospital.

Her blankets trailed behind him. One tumbled out of the car, lying crumpled on the pavement.

Chad followed. As he got through the doors, a blast of air conditioning hit him, followed by the smell of sterile air and disinfectants.

Hospitals. He thought he was shed of them that morning. And he'd only made things worse.

Michael had been led back into a large area with dozens of curtained beds and had put Katie on one bed. The nurses, along with an emergency room doctor, surrounded them. Michael was explaining what was happening, his hands moving.

"I'm her father," Chad said as he shoved up closer. "She's been sick a long time."

"What's the problem exactly?" the doctor demanded.

He was a young man, so young that Chad wondered how long he'd been practicing medicine. As he asked the question, he didn't even look at Chad. He was already examining Katie, trying to see what was causing her distress.

"The problem?" Chad repeated. "Well, that's what no one seems to know."

The doctor glanced up at him.

"It's a long story," Chad said.

"Let me get her stable first and then you can tell me," the doctor said. "Is she on any medications?"

"Not yet, thank God," Michael said.

Chad glared at him. "Yes," he said, and proceeded to tell the doctor what they were.

The nurses eased Michael out of the emergency room, pulling a curtain in front of him and telling him to go down the hall to wait.

Michael stood in front of the curtain for a long time, listening to Chad's litany of medications for a little girl dying of a mystery disease, the doctor's not-so-gentle questions, and Katie's miserable cough.

There was nothing Michael could do. He'd sat in that backseat, his arms wrapped around her, and thought of Max. All Max would have done was place his hand on her stomach and done that thing he'd done before, with the other kids. With Liz, the time she got shot at the Crashdown.

With all of them.

And Katie would have been saved. Instead, Michael had to trust a doctor who looked like he had just graduated from medical school and a father who had already proven his poor judgment.

Michael stood in the hallway for another moment. Behind a nearby curtain, he heard an elderly lady cry out in pain. A doctor's voice rose from yet another area, telling someone that everything would be all right. And a nurse went by, wheeling a machine that looked even scarier than Katie's blue face.

Michael didn't belong here.

"Excuse me, sir." The security guard came over. "I'm sorry to bother you right now, but your car is blocking the emergency entrance."

Michael stared at him for a moment, trying to process what the man said.

"Can you move it? Or give me permission to do so? We have an ambulance coming in a few minutes and they need to be able to park there."

"Um, sure," Michael said, and hurried outside.

The backseat door was still open, a blanket lying on the pavement beside the car. The driver's-side door was open, too, and the car was making a futile little beeping noise, telling the entire world that the door was open and the keys were still in the ignition.

The keys were in the ignition.

Newcomb was going to be in that hospital for a long time.

And those scum scam artists were supposed to meet him with the serum in just over an hour.

Michael glanced at the doorway, wondering if his thoughts were evident on his face. It didn't matter if they were. People looked worried around emergency rooms all the time.

He grabbed the blanket, threw it on the backseat, and slammed the back door. Then he went around to the driver's side. He slipped in, pulled the door closed, and grabbed the wheel.

It would be a long time before Newcomb knew the car was gone. Even if he asked about it, the guard would say that he'd told Michael to move the car. The nurse would say that Michael was in the waiting room.

Newcomb wouldn't know Michael was gone for an hour, maybe more. And then what could he say about it? Hey officers, the guy who stole my car was the same guy I kidnapped from Roswell, New Mexico?

Michael seriously doubted Newcomb was dumb enough to say that.

He put the car in drive, and headed out of the emergency area, going to the main part of the parking lot first, so that no one would think anything of what he was doing.

Max wouldn't know what to do when he got to the GasMart. Michael hadn't had a chance to explain anything to Maria, and as usual, she'd asked too many questions, and taken up too much time. Michael might have had a chance to explain if she hadn't asked so many questions.

He had to get to the meeting spot when the serum guy did. And he would have to play it as if Katie were his daughter.

He had a hunch people didn't usually bring their kids to this thing, and Newcomb had already paid the money. All Michael had to do was get the stuff, and find out where the guys were working from. Then he would come back to the GasMart, and he and Max and Tess and Isabel would take care of the scum once and for all.

Then, when it was all done, he'd bring Max here, to Katie.

Max would be able to help her then. All she had to do was survive another few hours.

Michael would get her her miracle. He wouldn't be able to live with himself otherwise.

14

March 24—Las Cruces, New Mexico

Nila pulled into a Texaco StarMart, stopping in front of the gas pumps.

"What's going on?" Max asked.

Those were the first words he'd spoken for the past fifteen miles. The kid could be silent as a stone. He sat in the seat beside her, staring straight ahead, as if he could get the car to move faster just by watching the road.

The girls in the backseat weren't much help, either. They sat as far from each other as possible, and both of them looked out their windows.

Nila thought teenagers were talkative, but this group proved that a myth. They'd hardly said five words to each other in the last hour.

"I need to stop," she said.

"Yeah, that's a good idea," Tess said from the back. She opened the door and was out of the car before Nila had it in park.

Cool air blew in. It had been unseasonably warm all day, so Nila had the air conditioner on. But it was twilight now, and the night chill was settling over the desert. Nila's jacket was in the trunk. She would have to get it before they left this stop.

"I thought we were in a hurry," Max said.

"We are." Nila took the keys out of the ignition. "But we have some needs to attend to—both mine and the car's, so if you don't mind."

He shrugged. For a moment, she thought he was going to continue staring straight ahead, like he had been doing all along. Then he got out of the car and walked to the pump.

"What do you take? Super unleaded?"

"Regular unleaded is fine," she said. And cheaper. She'd already spent enough on the company credit card.

He went to the tank and started to fill it, which was certainly not behavior she would have expected, given his attitude all day. She didn't remember being this weird when she was a teen. Her older brother had been surly; in fact, she couldn't remember him saying a kind word from the time he turned thirteen until he turned twenty.

But Max was quietly unpredictable. Just when Nila thought she had him figured out, he did something like fill her tank.

She got out of the car. It felt good to stretch her legs. She'd been driving for a little under three hours, and questioning her decision to bring these kids the entire way.

She hadn't even checked to see if they had told their parents where they were going. They were all minors. If even one of them made an accusation against her, she was in deep trouble, since she was taking them across state lines—or would be in a few more miles.

Maybe she should reconsider this whole thing.

She stepped across the pump island and headed toward the familiar red and black building. Nila didn't see Tess inside, which meant she had probably had to make the same stop Nila did.

Her stomach was rumbling, too. A bit of food, and then she'd be ready to tackle the remaining hours of the drive.

She glanced over her shoulder. Liz was following her, head down, purse clutched in one hand. Nila had no idea why Liz had come along. At first, she had thought it was the typical jealous female thing—she had to be in the same place as her boyfriend and Tess. But slowly, Nila realized that Liz and Max were uneasy with each other. She got the sense, from the little bits of discussion she heard, that the relationship was over.

So that theory was gone.

Then, a few miles later, she discovered that Max had asked Liz to come with them.

Nila couldn't figure that out. Liz didn't seem to have special skills. She wasn't as edgy as Tess, or as calm as Max. And although she was in good physical shape, she wasn't strong, either.

Nila grabbed the glass door and held it open for Liz. Liz gave her a tired smile as she walked through.

"So," Nila said, "you want to tell me what's up?"

"I don't know what you mean," Liz said.

"This afternoon, you were all worried about your friend Michael, so worried you weren't doing your job well. Now you're willing to come with me? Even force me to leave early."

Liz sighed. "Michael called. Some friends are going to pick him up."

"So he's all right?"

"We think so." That didn't sound positive.

"You think so?"

Liz nodded and headed toward the ladies' room. She tried the door, but it was locked. Tess was probably still inside.

Nila trolled a few of the aisles, looking for something that wasn't too fatty or salty. Of course, she was having no luck. She gave up and got behind Liz, forming a line near the ladies' room door.

"I understand you're a science wiz," Nila said.

Liz gave her a startled look. "What makes you think that?"

Nila smiled. "I'm a reporter. I spent two days in Roswell. I learn things."

"What kind of things?" Liz sounded nervous.

"You're a science wiz who used to date Max. Then Tess moves to Roswell and suddenly you're out in the cold."

"It's not like that," Liz said.

"Then what is it like?"

The bathroom door opened. Tess came out, her hair neatly combed. Nila had the feeling that she'd been listening.

Liz kept her head down and went into the ladies' room. Tess glared at Nila and walked out of the store.

Nila sighed. Every time she had opened conversational

gambits like that, they had fizzled. Three hours of non-starters. She was beginning to think she'd lost her touch.

But she knew better. She had realized from the moment she got into the car that she wasn't in control of this trip. Max was, and he managed it without saying a word.

Somehow she had to find out more about this kid. Did charismatic world leaders have this kind of effect when they were under twenty? Was it something people were born with? Or was she just susceptible to Max's charms the way that Tess and Liz were?

Nila glanced through the glass windows at the pumps. Max had finished filling up the tank. He was talking with Tess, gesturing as he did so. She nodded, then got into the car, closing the door.

She wasn't happy with him. Neither girl was. And Nila couldn't find out why.

Her best chance was Liz. She'd try talking with her again later. If it were necessary.

First and most importantly, Nila had to focus on what she was going to do when she got close to the scam artists' hideout. Was she going to trust Max and take him down that road?

Sooner or later he would have to talk to her. Before they got to Florence Junction.

Nila might not have controlled the trip so far, but she would control it there. She had to. She still wasn't sure what she was getting into, and she wasn't the kind of person who just charged blindly ahead.

She would have to know why Max was at the hospital before she took him to that dirt road. He didn't want to tell her, and that intrigued her most of all.

Maybe she would ask him about the silver handprint and see what his reaction was. Or maybe she'd ask him how a man impersonates an angel and then disappears out an open window.

She had to find something to rattle him, and she had to do it in the next two hours.

If she was creative, she would come up with something.

She always did.

15

March 24—Outside of Bensen, Arizona

Truck-stop heaven. Michael had forgotten how dry and dusty this place was. He had pulled into the GasMart's parking lot twenty minutes ago, and had been sitting in the exact location where he needed to be ever since.

He had parked in the outermost right-hand slot on the west side of the GasMart, exactly according to instructions. There were no windows on this side of the building—just a large Dumpster and a metal back door that had a big sign on it, declaring that the door was locked and any tampering would cause some security system to go off.

From this position, Michael could see the diner across the street. It did a lot of business, mostly trucks. Beside the diner was one of those really large truck stops, the kind that had beds and showers in the back for the long haul guys. There was a store attached to it, filled with all kinds of stuff, judging by what was in the windows.

On the other side of the GasMart, there were some fast-food places and one extremely cheap, somewhat scary-looking motel.

Traffic went by at a fast pace here, almost as if no one wanted to get caught driving through this area, let alone stopping. He understood why the serum guys had chosen this as a drop point. It was perfect. There were so many transient vehicles that two more wouldn't be noticed at all.

He wondered if that meant some local knowledge on their part or if they had just stumbled into this place as they were passing through.

Michael had the radio on softly to keep himself awake and the windows down, letting in the chill air. It was twilight, although it was kind of hard to tell. About the time he pulled in, all the lights had gone on at every business at the junction. Floods at the truck stop, neon at the diner, and good old-fashioned bulbs here at the GasMart.

All that brightness had nearly blinded him, and for a while, he wondered if he had missed his rendezvous.

But the truck stop across the street kindly displayed the time and temperature every thirty seconds. Michael had arrived early, and it was driving him crazy.

He had kind of hoped that Max and Isabel would have been here by now, but he knew that was wishful thinking. The drive from Roswell was a lot longer than the drive he had made—even with his almost hour-long detour at the hospital.

He wished Newcomb had had a cell phone in the car. Michael had searched for a phone after he stopped, but hadn't found one. He wanted to call Maria to find out where everyone was, and then he wanted to call the hospital for an update on Katie. She hadn't looked good when he left, and he had a bad feeling about it.

Newcomb might have been stupid, but Michael didn't think Katie should pay for her father's mistakes.

Michael knew there had to be pay phones in the truck stop across the street, but he didn't want to leave the car, not even for a minute. It would be just his luck that the serum guys would show up while he was trying to call Maria.

Besides, it was impossible to get her off the phone. Better to wait until later—if he got the chance.

Still, he was driving himself crazy waiting here. He had only the glimmerings of a plan. All he knew was that he had to stop these guys from making money off Max's miracle—off the fact that Max had done something good and noble.

These guys might even be accidentally killing kids with their phoney medicine—kids like Katie.

Michael shuddered.

At that moment, a truck pulled up beside him. It was an older one-ton like so many that went by on the road here, dented and scarred. Well-used and well-loved.

The truck had a gun rack in the back window, and a topper that looked like it had been purchased at a garage sale. The guy driving was huge and burly. He got out of the cab, whistling that obnoxious Shania Twain tune about impressing people. Michael had hated the song when it had dominated the radio a while back.

The guy left the cab's door open.

Michael got out, too, leaving his door open. The instructions had been clear on this part. He was so glad Newcomb had left the instructions in the car.

The guy wore a cowboy hat and boots, which added to his height. He towered over Michael.

"A little young to have a kid," the guy said.

A little dim to have invented a serum, Michael almost countered, but didn't. He wondered what Newcomb would have thought of this guy—what the other parents had thought. "Some of us start young."

"I guess," the guy said. He reached behind the driver's seat and pulled out an ice chest, shoving it toward Michael. Michael took it.

"So you invented this stuff?" he asked because he couldn't help himself.

The guy studied him for a minute. "The note said no questions."

"I'll bet I'm not the first person who asked you that," Michael said, as he adjusted his hands on the cooler. It wasn't heavy, just awkward.

"No, you're not," the guy said. He grinned and rocked back on his high-heeled boots. "I'm just the delivery service."

Michael nodded. "So you don't know how to work this stuff."

"There's directions inside the cooler. Read 'em carefully and follow 'em to the letter. Got that?"

"Yeah," Michael said. He had no idea why people would think this was legitimate, even if these guys had invented the world's greatest potion. Wouldn't they have a roadside stand or something? A redneck with a pickup truck and shoulders so broad he could carry the world on them didn't exactly inspire confidence.

But then, why would these guys be worried about confidence now? They already had the money. Technically they didn't have to deliver the stuff at all.

"Thanks," Michael said, and put the cooler in the backseat, where Katie's blankets were. They, more than anything, probably convinced the guy that Michael was for real.

"Sure thing," the guy said, touching the brim of his hat, and getting into the cab of his truck.

The moment the guy turned his back, Michael opened his palm. This was the tricky part. His powers were not finesse powers, and this was going to take some delicate work.

He imagined a tiny hole in the front tire and sent a little puff of energy toward it. The energy arrived in the form of a tiny fireball that burned right through the tire.

The smell of burning rubber mixed with all the exhaust and diesel fuel that seemed to permeate the air here.

The guy didn't seem to notice. He got into his truck and started the engine.

Michael got into the car, then leaned out the window. "Hey," he said, "did you know you have a flat?"

The guy frowned. The tire wasn't done decompressing, so he probably couldn't feel the tilt inside the truck yet. "What?"

Michael started his car and then pointed at the tire. "A flat!" he shouted at the guy over the engine sound. "On the front driver's side."

The guy frowned at him, obviously not willing to trust him.

"I'd help, but I have to get this stuff to my daughter.

Thanks for bringing it here," Michael said as he put the car in reverse and backed up.

Then he turned and peeled out of the lot, making it seem like he was in a great hurry. As he hit the road, he glanced into his rearview mirror.

The guy had gotten out of his truck and was prodding the flat tire with his toe.

Michael grinned and headed off the way he came, just in case the guy was watching him. He got on the freeway heading for Tucson, drove until the next exit, then got off and went over the overpass to a frontage road. A few moments later he was headed back to the truck stop.

When he got close, he parked in a fast-food restaurant parking lot. Fortunately Newcomb's car looked like every other car on the road. The guy wouldn't be able to tell that this car belonged to Michael.

He would think Michael was long gone.

Michael made sure he could see the GasMart and the truck from his parking place.

Then he settled in and watched as the big guy tried to figure out how to change a tire.

Maria pulled her phone out of her purse. The digital front declared that the phone was on and that it was in a service area. In fact the line that went up the right side of the face indicated that the phone was charged and receiving full power.

It just wasn't getting any calls.

"Staring at it won't make it ring," Alex said. He was sitting behind her, in the backseat of the van Sheriff Valenti had borrowed. "Unless, of course, you're Isabel."

"I can't make phones ring," Isabel said. She was sitting beside Alex and she looked vaguely annoyed at his comment.

She seemed as on edge as Maria felt. For several miles now, Maria had been wondering if she dreamed that phone call from Michael. The first time she pulled out her phone, she opened the digital memory and glanced at the call history.

Sure enough, she had gotten a call when she was at Michael's apartment. She hadn't made that up.

"I don't expect any calls for a while," Valenti said, glancing over at her as she put the phone away. He was driving easily, one hand on the steering wheel, the other resting on the floor shift. He was the only one, of all of them, who didn't seem nervous.

"Why not?" Isabel asked.

"It sounds like Michael called you in the middle of something," Valenti said. "He's not the type of guy who'll call whenever something changes."

"No kidding," Maria said.

"Max is," Isabel said.

"Yes, but I suspect Max has his hands full. I've read stuff by that reporter. She's even been on some of those news talk shows on Fox and MSNBC. She's good, and she's dogged."

Valenti glanced into the rearview mirror. He'd been doing that a lot. When Alex had asked him about it, Valenti had merely said, "Just checking."

"Great, a dogged reporter. That's all we need," Alex said.

"If I had been involved in the planning of all of this," Valenti said, "I wouldn't have recommended trusting her."

"We didn't trust her," Isabel said. "She threatened to expose Max and Michael to the Phoenix police."

Valenti let out a great sigh. Maria gave him a sideways glance. He looked very irritated. "You kids should have told me about the whole thing—at Christmastime."

"Well, we didn't—" Maria said.

"Because," Valenti said, interrupting her, "we could have done something then. *I* would have known about the security cameras in the hospital. We might have come up with a cover story."

He sounded more irritated than Maria had heard him sound since the trip to Las Vegas. He hadn't known about the Christmas Miracle until this afternoon, and he wasn't pleased about it.

"You kids are taking too many risks," he said. "Max and Michael have to know that. The more people who see you use your...powers...the more cover-up you have to do. Eventually, there will be a leak, and it'll be a dangerous one."

"Max is trying to cope with that now," Isabel said.

"So," Valenti said, "let's say he finds the men who are running this scam. Then what?"

Isabel shrugged. "Max will figure out what to do."

"That's what I'm afraid of," Valenti said. "And what happens if they find a list of all the families who bought this junk?"

"I don't know," Maria said. "Maybe they give it to the reporter."

"Maybe," Valenti said. "But that doesn't sound like Max, does it?"

"He won't risk trying to find all those children," Isabel said.

"Won't he? He risked everything on Christmas because, he said, he was seeing a ghost. How badly will this haunt him? Children getting harmed worse because of an opening he gave to some scam artists."

"It's not Max's fault," Maria said.

"I know that," Valenti said. "You know that. But we're talking about Max here."

"He can't do anything tonight," Alex said, trying to calm them all down. "I mean, even if he finds the guys, he can't do anything with the kids."

"And he's supposed to trust this reporter?" Valenti said.

"You're the one who said you recognized her name," Isabel said.

"I know," Valenti said. "I've just learned over the years not to trust any reporters, no matter what they promise."

"Maybe we should call him," Isabel said.

"And say what?" Maria asked. "Don't trust the lady? I think Max is bright enough to know that."

"It's all past tense now," Alex said. "Whatever happens happens."

"I didn't know you were such a fatalist," Isabel said to him.

He glanced at her and gave her a fond smile. Maria saw the reflection of it in the windshield.

"I guess I learned to accept a lot in the last couple of years," he said.

Isabel looked vaguely guilty and turned her head away from him. Valenti shook his head slightly.

"Do we know what Michael is doing at this junction?" he asked Maria for the fifth time.

"No," she said.

"I don't like this," Valenti said. "We don't know what we're getting into. And it sounds, from what you've told me, like Michael has picked up some friends—or they picked him up."

"No one can hold Michael for long," Isabel said.

"We don't know that," Alex said. "We've come across a few things that aren't safe for you guys."

"Do you think this is some sort of setup?" Maria asked Valenti. That had never crossed her mind. She'd thought of other possibilities, but never that someone was using Michael as bait.

"Yeah," Valenti said. "I think that's a distinct possibility."

"What would they want?" Isabel asked.

"Probably you, Max and Tess," Alex said.

"Michael didn't ask for that," Isabel said.

"Actually, he sort of did," Maria said.

There was silence in the car. Finally, Isabel said, "What do you mean?"

"He asked that we all meet him. I'm sure he wanted Max along. I'm sure he expected that Tess would come, too."

Valenti shook his head again. Sometimes he could be as annoying as Kyle. Up until this point, Maria hadn't thought they had much in common.

"Well," Isabel said. "All they'll get is me."

"They won't get that," Valenti said. "We're going into this thing prepared for the worst. All of us. You got that?"

Maria felt cold.

"Does that mean we should have a plan?" Alex asked.

"We can't have a plan if we don't know what's going on," Maria said.

"We have another couple of hours," Valenti said. "I'm sure we'll come up with something."

Isabel sighed and rested her head against the back of the seat. "How come things can't just be normal for even a few days?"

Alex grinned at her. "You'd get bored."

"I would not," Isabel said. "I like normal."

"Yeah," Maria said, as tension gnawed at the inside of her stomach. "Me too."

16

March 25—Florence Junction, Arizona

Nila took a sip from the cold mocha she'd bought two stops back. The caffeine and chocolate were working in her system, making her hyper and tense.

The road was dark. At times it seemed as if theirs was the only car on it. She'd had too many miles of silence to reflect on what she was doing. She shouldn't have listened to this Max kid. For all she knew, he was letting her think she was taking him to the scam artists when, in fact, he was actually bringing her.

At the last rest stop, a few miles back, she'd gone into the ladies' room and called the paper. Even though it had been after midnight, the production manager and the managing editor were still in, juggling headlines for the regular morning edition.

Nila had told them she was investigating a lead near Florence Junction, and that if she didn't call in by noon the next day, to send someone to look for her. That was the best she could do.

She had tried to leave the girls at a stop near where they left the freeway, telling Max it wasn't safe to bring them along. She had said that it would be better for them to sit inside, have a Coke on her, and wait. They had cell phones. It wasn't like she was abandoning them.

But Max had said no. He didn't want to be separated from them.

Nila had been quietly relieved. She didn't want to leave two girls alone, but she was at her wit's end. She wasn't sure what would be the best course right now. Right now, the kids outnumbered her and if they were working with the guys who made the serum, she could be in real trouble.

On the other hand, the kids might have special knowledge that would get her inside the scam artists' hideaway.

But neither of those things felt right. She got a sense of quiet fury from Max, and if the truth be told, she was a bit worried that he might just go a little crazy on her. Not against her. Against the scam artists.

And that wouldn't be good, either. From the looks of the guy in the pickup she had followed to find their hiding place, they were not people to mess with.

She turned onto the unmarked county road that led to the hideout.

"How much farther?" Liz asked.

"Not much," Nila said, then felt a surge of irritation. She answered their questions, but none of them had answered hers. No matter how innocuous the questions seemed—she'd even tried to draw them out about school—no one had really spoken to her with anything but surface answers.

She felt like a leper. A lot of people made her feel like that as a reporter, but she never thought a group of kids would be sophisticated enough to do it so young.

The unmarked dirt road showed up as a dark space against the two-lane highway. She wouldn't have seen it if she hadn't known it was there.

She parked and shut off her lights.

"You kids wait here," she said.

"No," Max said.

"Listen, I've already compromised enough," she said. "I have no idea what's down that road and I'm not risking your lives to find out."

"If something happens to you, then what?" Max asked.

She looked at him.

"You don't trust me, do you?" His voice was calm. Usually people were upset when they asked that question.

"Why should I? You won't tell me what your involvement is in all of this."

"You can trust me," he said. "Me, and Tess, and Liz. Right, Tess?"

"Right, Max," she said.

It was a strange interchange, and made Nila even more uneasy. "Generally, trust isn't commanded," she said. "It's earned."

"Have I done anything to break your trust?" Max asked.

"Yes," Nila said. "You haven't told me about the hospital."

"Maybe you haven't asked the right questions." He turned toward her, his features hidden in the darkness. "You ready?"

She thought she saw a nod from the backseat. "No way," she said. "I'm not taking all of you down that road."

"Just me," Max said. "Tess and Liz have phones. They'll call for help if we need it."

It sounded like a good enough plan. Nila sighed. "We're just going to see what's down there. We'll make plans after that."

"Fair enough."

They got out of the car together, and, in unison, closed the doors so quietly that they clicked. Nila's sensible shoes crunched the gravel on the turn-out. Somehow Max's tennis shoes made no sound at all.

Side by side they walked down the highway to the dirt road and then headed down it. It was easier to navigate than she thought it would be. There were just scrub and rocks alongside. The moon was almost full—she hadn't noticed that as she drove, and thought it odd that she'd notice it now—shedding a bright light across the landscape.

It was rough, cragged, and like most of the country south of Tucson, but for some reason the road seemed flat and seemed to go on forever.

Max glanced at her. "I don't like this," he said.

She didn't, either. Just from what she could see in the moonlight, they'd have to walk quite a distance and she wasn't sure what they'd find.

"This road could go on for miles," he said.

She hadn't had that impression the first time she came here, but then she hadn't driven down the dirt road.

"Maybe we should wait until dawn and drive as far as we can," Max said. "We might be able to see more then. And dawn isn't that far off."

They could see a lot now, but distances were hard to judge in the moonlight. She'd learned that years ago, on stakeouts with some cops.

"There's a hotel back a few miles," she said. "How about I drop you kids off there and I come back here?"

"No," Max said. "Let's just wait."

She looked out ahead. The road seemed to go on forever. The dirt was flat—hard-packed with no gravel—and if she was careful, she would be able to drive it without making much of a sound. Besides, it was wide enough for only one car. If the scam artists came back this way, she'd see them—or they'd see her.

She sighed. "I guess waiting won't hurt," she said.

Max nodded, and together, they headed back to the car.

It took a few minutes to get back up the road. When they reached the highway, Nila was surprised to find Tess standing at the road's entrance.

"I thought you were going to wait in the car," she said, more harshly than she had planned.

"I got worried," Tess said. "You were gone for a while."

They hadn't been—not really. And Tess didn't sound worried. Nila frowned at her, but said nothing as they headed back to the car.

Max told Tess the plan, and they all got into the car. Liz looked at them curiously, but didn't say anything.

Nila settled into her seat, and grabbed the Styrofoam cup holding her mocha. Good thing she'd bought the largest size possible. This was going to be a long night.

Max settled in beside her and stared straight ahead—as if he couldn't just see into the distance, but into the future as well.

She'd never seen a kid his age sit so still.

And she'd never sat on an Arizona highway that seemed so empty.

An almost full moon. How had she missed that?

She'd been off all day. She hoped this feeling would change before morning—or at least before dawn.

Max let out a small breath. He raised his eyes to the rearview mirror. Tess gave him a thumbs-up.

She looked distracted, still focusing on creating a false landscape to distract Nila. She had already put her energy into making that road look like it went on forever, tricking Nila's eyes, when it had actually curved through rocks and scrub and looked like a relatively short road. Max had thought he'd seen the outline of a house tucked up against a rock bluff ahead of where they had stopped. The faster Max scoped out the road, alone, the better off they'd all be.

Fortunately, Nila had disappeared into the ladies' room twice on this trip, so he and Tess had had time to plan that they would give Nila the "virtual" vision of a long quiet night. It would be hard for Tess to sustain, but she was determined.

Max glanced over his shoulder. Liz's eyes met his. She was going to stay in the car until he came back, mostly to keep an eye on Tess and distract Nila if the vision wavered.

He was quiet as he let himself out of the car. He closed the door so gently this time that the car didn't even rock. He made his way across the gravel toward the dirt road.

As he did, lights appeared in the distance. He ducked into a drainage ditch, and hoped that the passing car wouldn't notice Nila's car in the turn-out. Maybe if the driver did, he might think that Nila was sleeping. Folks did that in turn-outs in the desert, trying to take care of themselves on long difficult drives.

The drainage ditch was empty, the ground hard and dry. The air smelled faintly of oil, sage, and a plant that Max couldn't identify.

The car got closer, the sound of its engine impossibly loud in the night silence. Finally he caught a glimpse of the vehicle and realized it was too large to be a car. It was some kind of truck.

Then, as he watched, it slowed.

His heart pounded. The driver was going to stop and investigate the car in the turn-out. That was not what they all needed.

Headlights swept over him, and he ducked, praying that the driver didn't see him. The truck turned on the dirt road. Dust and gravel sprayed up behind its wheels. Some small rocks hit Max on the back, but he didn't care.

His breath caught in his throat.

It was one of the scam artists, heading back to the house.

He would have someone to follow.

He waited until the taillights disappeared in the scrub before clambering up the side of the drainage ditch. As he did, he realized that the engine noise hadn't faded.

There was another car on the road, only this car had its lights out. Max didn't like that at all. Nothing good came of cars driving with their lights out.

Except that the driver hadn't seen him yet.

The car pulled onto the shoulder on the opposite side of the dirt road from Nila's car and about a hundred paces short. There was a chance, in the dark, the driver hadn't seen Nila's car yet.

Max wondered what Liz and Tess thought of all this. He hoped it wasn't distracting Tess enough to force her to drop her control of Nila's vision.

That was the last thing they needed.

The car's engine shut off, plunging the night back into intense desert silence, then the driver's door opened.

Max stayed frozen in place. A single movement might call attention to him.

The driver stepped out, and as he did, Max let out the breath he'd been holding.

The driver looked familiar. In fact, Max would recognize that walk anywhere. He'd seen it his entire life.

The car's driver was Michael.

Okay, so driving with his headlights off wasn't the brightest thing he'd ever done. For one thing, it was harder than he had expected it to be.

He'd done it in Roswell on one regrettable night when some guys from school had talked him into playing car tag. He'd spent maybe five minutes driving with his lights out, decided it was stupid, and quit the game.

But driving then hadn't seemed so difficult. The city's streetlights had provided more than enough light.

On this night, out here, the road was pretty dark. Once the truck had turned off, he had a heck of a time seeing anything ahead of him. He almost missed the dirt road and somehow managed to get the car stopped without putting it into the ditch.

The entire night's drive had been one comedy of errors

after another. He'd waited behind that fast-food joint for nearly an hour while the truck driver had struggled to fix his flat. At one point, Michael had nearly gotten out of his car and gone to help him, the guy was so bad at it.

A guy who looked as tough as that driver should have known how to change a tire. There was just no telling with people.

Then when the driver had finished with the tire, he'd gone into the GasMart to wash up. He'd come out, and Michael had started his car, expecting to get on the road.

Instead, the driver had driven across the street to the diner, parked in the back, and gone inside.

Michael had had to drive to the truck stop across the street and hide his car among the big rigs. From there, he could see inside the diner. A big-chested waitress, with red hair that was so uniformly perfect that it had to be a wig, flirted with the truck driver while he ate the biggest burger Michael had ever seen.

Then the waitress had called to another waitress in the back, and disappeared out the side door with the driver.

Michael watched as they got into the truck. The cab's windows had fogged up and fortunately, he hadn't been able to see anything at all. He was going to assume, for his sanity's sake, that they were talking.

He didn't want to think that they were doing anything else.

After an hour, the waitress got out of the truck, blew the driver a kiss, and headed back inside the diner.

Then, and only then, had the driver taken off.

While he waited, Michael kept hoping Max and the others would arrive, but they hadn't. They really didn't have much of a chance to get there. He'd contacted Maria just before he left with Newcomb, and even with the stop at the hospital, he still had gotten to the junction hours before they would.

Even with all the goofing around, the driver had wasted only a couple of hours.

Still, if Maria had gathered everyone together, and they had left at the same time, they might have arrived at the junction before he left, if whoever was driving really pushed it.

Leave it to Maria to slow everyone down.

They would be there when he got back—whenever that would be. The driver had left the junction quickly, but had taken his time after that. He didn't seem to care about the speed limit, often going slower than usual, as if he were looking for something. He stopped twice, both times to pick up beer at convenience stores along the road.

But he did put the beer into the back of the truck, so Michael knew he wasn't drinking it. He also carried out paper sacks filled with groceries, or supplies of some kind. Michael had no idea why the guy didn't get everything at a real grocery store, but then, Michael didn't understand people who ripped off sick and dying kids for a living.

Michael made sure he stayed as far back as he possibly could. The driver never once turned around, so Michael didn't think the guy had made him.

Still, it paid to be cautious. Who knew what was at the end of all this? Yes, Michael had powers and the guy in the truck probably didn't, but Newcomb had proven that sometimes powers were worthless, especially if someone surprised Michael.

He didn't even have a phone to call anyone for help. This time, it was just him.

He wasn't sure he liked that.

Michael got out, blinded by the car's interior dome light for a moment, as the door opened. Then he moved down the shoulder of the road.

His eyes were adjusting quickly to the darkness, and ahead he realized that the blob in the darkness was another car. His stomach twisted. Did the car belong to one of the scam artists? Had they seen him coming?

Then he saw movement near the dirt road.

A man walked toward him.

"Michael," a familiar voice said. "It's me."

"Max?" Michael heard the uncertainty in his own voice. How had Max found him here?

And why?

How would Max know about this place?

"Keep it down," Max whispered as he approached him, moving very quietly across the gravel. "Tess is trying to focus in the car, and sound carries out here in the desert."

"Whose car is that?" Michael asked.

"There was a reporter in Roswell. She has a security video of us in the hospital. She's working on a story about some scam that someone is doing off the December twenty-fourth thing, and so she brought us here."

"Deliberately? Why would anyone do that?"

Max looked toward the car. "She thinks it'll help with her story."

"Did a snow job on her, huh, Maxwell?"

"No, that's what Tess is doing now. The reporter still

thinks I'm in the car, but I don't know how long Tess can keep this up. So I don't have a lot of time."

Michael looked toward the road. "I don't think either of us have a lot of time."

"You were following the guy, huh?" Max asked. "How did you know about this?"

"It's a long story, Maxwell. Better suited to an evening of soda and pizza than standing here in the dark. We've got to get down there and stop those guys."

"So it is a group of scam artists?"

"I don't know how many," Michael said. "But one of them is big enough to make Schwarzenegger nervous."

"Then we'd better be prepared," Max said.

Michael had had a long drive to think about what he'd do once he got to the scam artists' hidey hole. "Oh, I'm more than prepared, Maxwell. I'm ready to put an end to this once and for all."

17

Leave it to Michael to pick a place filled with trucks, junk, and no clear-cut meeting place.

Maria stepped into the Pie 'N' Stuff diner, and marveled at the smell. Pies, yes, but grease too, and aftershave. Apparently all diners did not smell alike.

Nor did they look alike. This one had windows on three sides, with a counter running down the middle and a kitchen that seemed to take up half the space. Men with greasy hair and bolo ties sat at the tables, and more men sat at the counter; beside them sat big pots of the darkest coffee Maria had ever seen.

Michael was not in here. She could tell that from first glance. Still, she had to go through the motions, like everyone else.

They had arrived at the junction about fifteen minutes ago, and stared at the buildings in dismay. Maria counted five fast-food restaurants, a very cheap-looking run-down motel, a super-duper truck stop that seemed to have everything except an auditorium, and the GasMart that Michael had mentioned.

Michael wasn't in or near the GasMart, and Valenti had used that as his excuse to get annoyed. He seemed to think it was someone's fault—Maria's, Isabel's, Alex's—that Michael hadn't given out enough information about the meeting place. Valenti had taken it as a personal affront that they now had to search for the elusive Michael Guerin.

Again.

So Maria had volunteered for the diner, since she was good at chatting up people. Alex and Isabel took the super-duper truck stop, since Valenti didn't want anyone going in there alone, and Valenti himself took all of the fast-food joints.

Alex had watched him go, and laughed, saying maybe Valenti was hungry.

They had left the van Valenti had borrowed in front of the GasMart. Isabel said Michael might recognize it because of the plates and the sheriff's sticker.

Maria had her doubts. Sometimes she wondered if Michael recognized her. He couldn't be relied on to recognize a van out of context in front of a 24-hour gas and convenience store.

"Help you?" the waitress asked. She was older than Maria's mom, and wore way too much makeup. Her foundation was too dark, and her eye shadow too green. She even had on false eyelashes, which Maria had never actually seen someone wear outside of a theater.

"Um, yeah," Maria said. "I'm looking for a friend of mine. He said to meet him here."

The waitress took a step closer and lowered her voice. "Honey, you don't want to wait here. Not without a friend or two watching you, if you know what I mean."

Maria felt a shiver run down her back. "I know. I have some friends over at the truck stop next door, and one of my friend's dad is across the street. We're all looking for the same guy."

"I thought you said he was going to meet you here."

"Here being the junction. He just didn't say where here."

"Oh," the waitress said. She frowned, as if she were concentrating. "What's he look like?"

"He's got brown hair, combed back away from his face and—oh, wait." Maria rummaged in her purse. She had a picture of Michael that she'd taken on their trip to Las Vegas. "This is him."

She shoved the picture at the waitress, who stared at it for a long time. "Your boyfriend?" she asked at last.

"I guess you could say that," Maria said.

"And he's missing?"

"No. He called this afternoon and said for all of us to meet him here."

"I've never seen him before, hon, but I just came on. Let me ask."

And before Maria could stop her, the waitress took the photo toward the counter. "Cinda, you seen this guy?"

Another waitress poked her head out the kitchen door. She wore a smooth red wig that was slightly askew. She held a cigarette in her left hand.

"What do you want, Diane? I'm getting ready to leave."

"Just look at this picture and tell me if you seen this guy."

"Why?" the other waitress asked.

"Because this girl here has misplaced her boyfriend," Diane said, looking over her shoulder.

"Yeah, haven't we all?" Cinda said.

"Except you, Cinda," Diane said. "C'mon. I saw you with that guy tonight."

Cinda gave her a slow smile and then a single shoulder shrug. "Some nights are better than others."

She took the photo from Diane and looked at it, then looked at Maria. "Hon," she said—"hon" was, apparently, a common nickname around these parts—"you shouldn't be chasing after a guy like this so late at night."

"Like you're one to talk, Cinda," said a guy at the counter.

"I am one to talk, Larry. Why'd you think I'm working here? Because I like the company?"

"Well, yeah."

Cinda shook her head and directed her next comment at Maria. "I wouldn't be here if it weren't for guys like this and their tendency to run off when they find out they're about to get an instant family. I didn't plan to waitress the rest of my life."

Neither did Maria, but she had a hunch now was not the time to say that. Nor was it the time to say that she had a similar job, just in a better place, with less grease.

"Have you seen him?" Maria asked. "It would have been sometime tonight."

"Nope, can't say as I have," Cinda said, "but I haven't been paying much attention tonight. Most everyone in here is something of a regular—you know, folks who drive through and make sure they stop here for the coffee or the pie."

She tapped the photo with one long, fake, glittery nail.

"But you know, I'd remember this guy. He's kinda cute."

"Yeah," Maria said, grabbing the photo. "He is."

Diane was watching her with a grin. "Well, show that picture around, hon. We're not the only pair of eyes in this place."

Maria did, somewhat reluctantly. She was glad she worked at the Crashdown where most of their customers were tourists or locals. She hadn't seen this much hair oil—not gel like Michael used—in one place at one time, maybe ever.

It took her a while to make it around the room, but by the time she was done, it was clear no one had seen him. And since she didn't know how he was coming here—whether by car or truck or some other means—she couldn't ask about that, either.

When she was done going around the diner, she thanked everyone. Cinda had disappeared into the back and a faint trace of cigarette smell told Maria that Cinda was finishing her smoke.

"Thanks," she said to Diane as she made her way to the door. "If he comes in here, would you tell him that we're all here and waiting for him?"

"I'll do just that, honey," Diane said. "You be careful now, okay?"

"Okay." Maria backed out the door into the cool night. She hadn't been nervous before she went into that place. Now she was seeing creeps hiding in shadows everywhere.

She didn't even look at the cars in the diner's parking

lot like she was supposed to. Instead, she wanted to find Isabel and Alex or Sheriff Valenti. Anyone, so she wasn't on this neon covered highway all by herself.

It seemed to take forever to cross the parking lot at the truck stop. She headed for the side entrance, until she saw a scrawny truck driver coming out, his hair wet, his shirt off, his jeans unsnapped, and a damp towel wrapped around his neck.

She didn't even say excuse me. Instead, she hurried to the front entrance where she almost ran into Alex and Isabel. They were coming out, looking very discouraged.

"No Michael, I take it," Maria said.

"Not that we could find," Isabel said.

"You know there's showers and stuff back there." Maria waved her hand in the general area of that trucker.

"No, I didn't." Isabel looked surprised. She glanced at the other entrance. "Maybe Alex should—"

"Alex will not. There are places that sane people do not go, no matter what's happening," Alex said. "If anyone goes, it'll be Sheriff Valenti. And maybe we'll convince him to take his gun."

"It can't be that bad," Isabel said.

Maria shuddered, thinking of the half-dressed truck driver. "Alex has pretty good instincts," she said.

"No Michael at the diner?" Isabel asked.

"Nope, but I didn't check the parking lot very well. It's spookier here than I thought."

"Let's do a check together," Alex said.

They started to walk around the parking lot, peering at cars to see if anyone was in them. Maria didn't know what they'd do about the long-haul trucks. If Michael was in one of those, they'd never find him. He'd have to find them.

"Where's the sheriff?" Isabel asked.

Alex pointed toward the motel. The sheriff's van was now parked under the streetlight, and through the open window in the well-lit manager's office, Maria could make out Valenti's back. He was gesturing toward the rooms, and the woman behind the desk kept shaking her head.

"Doesn't look like he's having a lot of luck," Maria said.

"I don't think Michael would be there," Isabel said. "It's not his style."

"Oh, I think it's just his style," Maria said. "A place with a bedroom that hasn't seen clean sheets since the *Titanic* sank."

"I wonder if he even knew what this place looked like," Alex said. "I mean, Michael's usually pretty specific about stuff."

"When it's important to him," Maria said.

"This is important to him," Alex said. "He wanted us here for a reason."

"He said the GasMart, right?" Isabel said.

"I think so, but there's no one there." Maria looked across the street. The GasMart was the only place without a car in the parking lot. She found that unnerving all by itself.

"He's just not here yet," Alex said. "I think we need to be patient."

"And wait, right?" Maria asked. There was more of an edge to her voice than she'd planned on.

Alex raised his eyebrows. "It's not my fault that you two have scheduling conflicts, Maria."

"You're the only guy here," Maria said. "Who else can I blame?"

There was no one in the cars around them, and no one in the diner's parking lot, either. The customers inside the diner hadn't changed.

Maria sat on a bench outside the diner. She was tired. She'd been up since early that morning, and her entire day had been focused on Michael Guerin. Maybe the waitress—Cinda?—was right. It was time to start concentrating on herself instead of focusing on a man.

She reached inside her purse and pulled out her cell phone. It was still working and still had power.

Then she stared at it, realizing what she had done. She had vowed not to focus on Michael while she was checking to see if he had called.

She had it bad. She used to tease Liz about the way she felt about Max, but it was nothing compared with all the time Maria had wasted on Michael.

Alex put a hand on her shoulder. His touch was comforting, just like his friendship was. "Don't worry," he said softly. "He'll be here."

"Soon, I hope," Isabel said.

"Yeah," Maria said, trying to sound tough. "This was not how I planned to spend my weekend."

"Oh, I don't know," Alex said, sitting beside her. "Hanging out at the diner, talking to friends. Isn't that how you always spend your weekend?"

Maria smiled in spite of herself.

"You're not helping, Alex," Isabel said.

"It's okay," Maria said.

At that moment, Valenti pulled up and leaned out the window of the van. "Anything?"

The three of them shook their heads.

"Me, either." He looked grim.

"What's the plan, sheriff?" Isabel asked.

He glanced at all of them. "Right now, there is no plan," he said. "I guess we just wait."

"Oh, goodie," Maria said. "Wait for Michael. Like I've never done that before."

18

March 25—Florence Junction, Arizona

Jerry sat at the table. The main room was dark except for the light coming from the computer screen. When Dane was gone, Jerry made sure he kept the place dark so that it didn't look like anyone was here. It would be hard enough to defend the place with only two guys.

It was nearly impossible with one.

He scanned the e-mails. Fifteen more people had e-mailed him. They'd found the web site and were writing for help.

He couldn't read the letters anymore. The sob stories were starting to get to him. Sometimes they made him mad—like who cared that some kid couldn't sleep through the night because he was in too much pain? Was that any of Jerry's business, really?—and sometimes they got to him.

Until he started this scam, he didn't think there was

anything that could get to him anymore. But he had been wrong.

If even ten of these fifteen came through, he and Dane would reach their money goal. And then they'd be done.

Not a moment too soon. Jerry wasn't sure he had the stomach for this anymore.

The sound of an engine grew in the distance. It sounded like Dane's truck, but Jerry wasn't sure. He put the computer on sleep mode and grabbed the gun he kept beside it. Then he walked toward the window.

He and Dane had discussed defense plans a hundred times. Dane had contended that anyone who drove down this road had no idea what—or who—was waiting at the other end.

Jerry had disagreed, often loudly. The cops would drive down the road. They wouldn't think that two guys could take them. They'd make as much noise as they wanted.

The argument never really was settled.

Jerry peered out the window. The night was darker than he liked and his eyes still hadn't adjusted. He squinted, saw the familiar shape of Dane's truck as a darker blob against the night sky. Jerry waited until it was a little closer, just to confirm, and then he went back to his spot near the computer.

The truck pulled up and stopped. The engine shut off and almost simultaneously, the truck door slammed.

Dane was moving faster than usual.

His boots clomped on the front porch and then he opened the main door.

"Jer?" he asked, softly.

"Right here," Jerry said. He didn't like the way this was going. "What's up?"

"You had problems tonight?"

"No, why?"

"There's a car in the turn-out, parked, with its lights off."

Jerry cursed. "You think they know about us?"

"Can't tell. Think maybe they might just be sleeping it off, you know? But I don't know for sure. Thought I'd tell you first."

Let the brains deal with it, Jerry thought. Good. He'd trained Dane better than he'd realized.

"There was also a guy in the ditch, but he could've been taking a whiz," Dane said. "I didn't get a good look at him."

"A guy in the ditch?" Now that was an unusual piece of information.

"Yeah, but like I said, I didn't get a good look at him. I did look in my rearview as I drove here, though, and he didn't follow me."

"At least by car."

"Well, I didn't see him on foot, either."

Jerry resisted the urge to shake his head. Dane might see that and take offense. "You would have been moving faster than he was if he walked."

"I mean, getting on the road." Dane's tone bordered on irritated.

"All right." Jerry's heart was pounding. He didn't like this news at all. He knew the next question would bother Dane, too, but he had to ask it. "So, were you followed?"

"I'm not an idiot!" Dane wheeled toward him. It was

at that moment that Jerry realized Dane had his gun out.

Jerry held up his hands just like people did in old movies. "I wasn't saying you were, Dane. Just checking everything."

"Besides, smart-ass, if I was being followed, the car wouldn't have gotten here ahead of me and parked with its lights out."

"True enough," Jerry said.

Which begged the question then. Just what was a car doing there?

And had Dane been followed before?

"I stopped twice on the way back, and I would've seen if the same car was behind me. Not to mention that it would've been pretty obvious on the highway this late."

"Yes, it would." Jerry hadn't brought his arms down. Dane was a little too on edge for him. "That was a dumb question. I shouldn't've asked it."

"Damn straight," Dane said.

Jerry eased his hands down. "The car that was parked there, and the guy…"

He let his voice trail off. He was going to take this next part slow.

"Yeah?" Dane asked.

"They saw you turn, right?"

"Yeah."

"They might not have known there was a road here before that."

"So?"

"So maybe they might want to explore it."

Dane didn't move for a long moment. "You're paranoid, you know that?"

"Yes," Jerry said.

"I mean, you say I worry too much, but you act like everything's going to go wrong."

"So you don't mind if some stranger comes down here and asks for a drink of water."

Dane cursed. "I was hoping for some sleep."

"Me, too," Jerry said.

"But you're a lousy shot."

"Yes," Jerry said. At least Dane had believed that lie.

"So I've got to sit on the porch all night and see if anyone comes down the road."

"We can both do it," Jerry said.

"Oh, yeah, like that'll work. You'll talk to me, and then we'll get distracted, and we'll miss whatever it is that you think's gonna happen."

"We can both do a perimeter search first," Jerry said. "Then I'll come back in and finish some work on the computer."

"Away from the window," Dane said.

"Right," Jerry said.

"Okay." Dane frowned at him. "Let's go."

He headed back toward the door. Jerry waited just a moment, checking his gun. His stomach was jumping. He didn't like how any of this sounded.

He should have known better than to trust Dane. Who knew what Dane had told that waitress? Or his buddies along the route? Dane had opinions and he liked to share them, and sometimes when he did, he used facts from his own life to back them up.

Dane looked over his shoulder. "You coming? Because if you're not, you'd better tell me. Or if you plan to do something else, you should tell me that, too. I see someone sneaking around the house, I'm not gonna ask if it's you. I'm gonna shoot. You got that?"

"Of course I do." Jerry took a deep breath. "I'm following you."

"Good," Dane said, and pulled the door open.

There wasn't enough scrub, and the rocks along the side of the dirt road didn't give the right kind of cover to hide behind.

Max scurried down the road, trying not to go too fast. There was a steep decline, and he was worried about sliding down it and making a lot of noise.

Michael didn't seem worried about the noise at all. In fact, Michael seemed more focused than usual, his gaze forward, his expression intense.

Max had only seen Michael like that a few times—and none of them had been good. At least for the people he directed that energy against.

They hadn't really discussed a plan. Michael said they didn't need one. But Max was uncomfortable taking orders from Michael—apparently whenever there was trouble they really did fall into the leader and general roles they'd had on their planet. And a leader didn't take orders from his general. Advice, yes, but not orders.

Max had tried to talk to Michael about a plan and Michael wouldn't listen.

"This isn't your battle, Maxwell," Michael had said.

Max had tried to argue, but Michael had shushed him.

"You don't know what I've been through the past twenty-four hours," Michael said. "These guys are mine."

Somehow, with Michael acting with that much determination, Max was unwilling to argue with him. He'd let Michael take the lead, as uncomfortable as that made him, although he did exact two promises from Michael.

First, Max wanted to make certain no one got killed. Michael didn't answer that one directly.

"We'll do what it takes, Maxwell. If they try to hurt you, then they answer to me."

That seemed fair enough.

The other promise was also important, though. Max wanted all the information on the serum and the people who were scammed. When he said that, Michael had looked at him.

"We're stopping this all the way," Michael said, "and that means letting people know they've been taken. So yeah, we get all the stuff."

Max didn't tell him that the fake meds also went to the reporter. It would have been one thing too many for Michael, and it was unnecessary at this point.

They just had to survive the next few minutes.

Max rounded the corner at the bottom of the decline and saw a house, tucked in against the rocks. The house looked dilapidated even in this poor light.

The truck he had seen a few minutes before was parked outside, its engine ticking. He thought he heard voices, speaking quickly, as if they were having an argument just inside the door.

Michael gave him a signal to follow. Max wasn't sure when Michael got ahead of him.

They had just made it around the truck when the front door opened. A man the size of a tree came out, a gun in his hand. Another, smaller man stood behind him.

"That's him," Michael whispered, but Max wasn't sure which man Michael was referring to.

It didn't matter. The large man saw Max and Michael, and raised his gun.

19

March 25—Florence Junction, Arizona

Liz shifted in the backseat. Tess was concentrating so hard beside her that she seemed to be vibrating.

Nila was staring straight ahead, unmoving. Liz wasn't sure if that was Nila's reaction to what Tess was doing or if that was what she'd be doing normally while she waited.

All this silence was driving Liz crazy, and she couldn't do much about it. Tess had carefully explained to her that she wasn't going to be part of the illusion. That whatever she did in the backseat might register for Nila. Tess wasn't sure how long Max was going to be gone, and she didn't want to use too much energy making certain Nila didn't follow him.

If Liz got out of the car, Nila would know.

But neither Tess nor Nila seemed to register the presence of the other cars—the truck that had turned down the lane with its lights on, driving as if it always went that way, and the car that pulled up shortly thereafter with its lights off.

Max had hidden in a ditch when the truck showed up and had gotten out after the second car parked. Then he talked to the other driver. They were too far away for Liz to see them clearly in the dark, and she couldn't hear anything they said.

She couldn't even risk opening a window to try to listen, and she didn't dare talk to Tess for fear of breaking her concentration.

But what if the second driver had pulled a gun on Max? What if Max was in trouble? How would she know?

She had to trust that he could take care of himself, that he wouldn't do anything foolish. But she wasn't comfortable with any of this. Sitting quietly in the dark while Tess made an illusion for Nila in the front seat was just not Liz's style.

Still, she knew better than to take matters into her own hands. It would make things worse, no matter how much she wanted to get out of the car.

She had to hold herself in place and concentrate on nothing. It was critical.

And she managed to do it for a good half hour after Max disappeared down the road.

Her ears were trained on each and every sound. She didn't move, and concentrated as hard as she could on everyone remaining safe.

On controlling herself and her impulses.

She clenched her hands together and held them in her lap, her fingers squished together.

A moment later, a series of loud bangs echoed in the silence. Gunshots?

She couldn't tell in the desert and the closed-up car. But they sounded like gunshots.

It took all of her willpower to stay in the car. And if something didn't happen fast, she wasn't going to much longer.

Jerry's fingers slid on the grip of his gun. He was sweating despite the chill of the evening. He was no good at this cloak-and-dagger stuff. Give him a computer and an idea, and he would do just fine.

But walking into a situation holding a gun made him realize just how stupid his life had become.

Dane stepped out the front door and stopped. He cursed under his breath and raised his gun.

Jerry's breath caught in his throat.

Suddenly the world exploded. Dane flew backward at him, his gun firing as he came.

It all seemed to be happening in slow motion.

Jerry tried to get out of the way of the flying body of the huge man, but he didn't have a chance. Dane slammed into him, and they flew backward into the wall between the front area and the kitchen.

Jerry hit first, so hard that his jaw snapped closed.

Pain radiated from his neck down his body.

It all registered fast, so fast that he knew he had no chance of fighting the unconsciousness that was sneaking over him.

Although he tried.

He really tried.

Max stared at the raised gun. This huge guy was going to shoot them for no apparent reason. This, more than anything, confirmed that they had found the right place.

Max started to raise his hand to make the protective energy shield. He'd stopped bullets with it before. But before he could face his palm forward, Michael's hand went up.

From it flowed light and energy so strong that Max could feel the edges of it. The light focused like a laser at the big guy, hitting him so hard that it pushed him backward with the force of an explosion.

The guy's gun went off twice, the sound echoing impossibly loudly in the desert and rocks.

And then Max couldn't see the guy anymore.

"What was that?" Max snapped.

"Sometimes you have to be ready to take action, Maxwell," Michael said, sounding calmer than he should have.

Max ran forward. He had said no killing and then Michael had done this. Michael was right behind him, guarding his back, apparently worried that there were more of them.

Max took the porch steps in one leap, and stopped in front of the open door.

The big guy had smashed the smaller guy into the wall. They were both unconscious—and both breathing.

But judging from the position of their legs, they weren't going anywhere soon. One of the big man's legs looked as if someone had bent it up and touched the back of his head with it. His gun was on the floor under the table.

Max wasn't about to heal them, not until he found out who they were.

"They may have others," Michael said, referring to the guns.

"You check them," Max said. "I'll look for rope."

He flicked on a light, revealing a main room filled with garage sale furniture and an old dining room table. On top of the table was an expensive new computer.

He glanced at the computer, but didn't go there—yet. Instead he went into the old-fashioned kitchen. On the table were bottles, some labeled, some not. Dirty dishes were piled in the sink, and empty TV dinner cartons lined the counters.

An open tool box stood on the floor, and inside it, along with another gun, was rope, more than enough to tie up the guys in the front room.

Max grabbed it, leaving the gun behind, and walked back to Michael. Together they tied up the men.

"You're sure this is the guy?" Max asked, staring at the broken form of the big man. He had blood running from a gash on his cheek, and there was no doubt he wouldn't be walking for a long, long time.

Michael nodded. "I don't want you helping them, Maxwell."

"I'm not even tempted," Max said.

Michael stood and stared into the room. "Now what?"

"You search. I'll see what I can find on that computer." Max headed toward the dining room table. "Be careful. I already found another gun."

"I checked. They don't have any more on them."

"Good," Max said.

Michael headed toward the kitchen.

"And don't touch anything unless you have to," Max said. "We want the cops to find this just as it is."

"Don't worry, Maxwell," Michael said. "If I need to pick something up, I put my hand in my sleeve, just like in the movies."

He said all of that with a straight face. He wasn't joking. He would do just that.

And Max had to do the same thing while working on the keyboard. No fingerprints. No sign that they were there.

Except Max wanted two things, and he knew they'd show up on the computer's hard drive. First, he wanted a list of all the people hurt by this scam, and then he wanted to see if anyone else was involved besides these two men.

He grabbed a super-disk and downloaded the entire hard drive. While the computer chugged away, Michael paced from room to room, his face getting grimmer.

"Those bottles look like the ones they gave me," he said. "And I found the money."

"Leave it," Max said. "Maybe the police can figure out who it belongs to."

"Don't worry," Michael said. "One illegal trip to Las Vegas is more than enough for me."

Max grinned in spite of himself, remembering the trip they took to get rid of the $50,000 Michael had been given by his real family. Blood money, Michael had said, in every sense of the word.

Rather like this stuff was.

Michael stopped beside him. "What are you doing?"

"Just getting some stuff," Max said.

"Wipe that keyboard clean."

"Don't worry," Max said.

"How long is this going to take?"

"Another few minutes," Max said. "I'm downloading the entire hard drive."

Michael shook his head. "For that reporter of yours?"

"No," Max said.

"She's our next problem, you know."

"No, she's not," Max said. "She is our key out of this."

Michael frowned at him, clearly not understanding.

Max stood. He had to take care of this anyway. "Stay here, make sure the computer doesn't freeze, and keep an eye on those guys."

"Why?" Michael asked.

"I'm going to get the reporter."

"Not a good idea, Maxwell."

Max smiled at him. "Actually, it's the best one I've had all day."

20

March 25—Florence Junction, Arizona

"**M**ax," Liz said. "Thank heavens you're all right."

All right? Nila shook her head. She felt like she was waking from a deep sleep. Why wouldn't Max be all right? He was sitting right next to her.

Only he wasn't.

He was outside the car, and Liz was hugging him. Tess had gotten out of the car and was going to his side.

Had Nila fallen asleep? Everything looked different. The moon was gone and the sky was dark, the way it got just before the sun started to rise.

She rubbed her eyes, not feeling like herself at all. Then she glanced at the mocha. Had those kids spiked it somehow? Over-the-counter sleeping pills really knocked her out.

That would have been a dangerous thing to do, but not something she would have put past Max Evans. He would have done it after they got to this place, then waited for her to fall asleep before going down to the house.

And confronting those scam artists?

Or helping them escape.

Nila cursed and got out of the car. "What's going on?"

Max looked over at her above Liz's head.

Tess stood beside him, and seemed both tired and smug.

Max slipped out of Liz's hug and walked toward Nila.

He nodded over his shoulder down the road. Nila looked in the direction he indicated and saw another car. It had clearly been parked there for a long time, and she had somehow missed it.

"What are you doing?" she asked.

"Michael got here a little while ago," Max said. "You were already asleep so we decided to go down to the cabin ourselves."

"Asleep?" She shivered. She didn't like the confirmation of her suspicions. "How far is the cabin? When you and I walked down there, we couldn't see anything."

Max frowned at her. "You said you wanted to close your eyes for just a minute when we stopped. I realized you were asleep when the truck went down the driveway and you didn't even notice. Michael was right behind him."

She blinked, confused. She never fell asleep on a stake-out. She'd once sat with cops for two days. They'd had relief, but she hadn't. And she'd managed to be awake the entire time.

She'd felt awake this time. She'd had enough caffeine and sugar to keep her fueled for days—unless he'd put something in that coffee like she suspected. She'd have to have it checked out when she got back to Phoenix.

"Michael and I managed to tie up your scam artists," Max said. "Come on. There's some stuff down in that cabin you need to see."

"Wait a minute," Nila said. "Why should I believe this wasn't just staged for my benefit? That you're somehow in league with these guys?"

Max gave her that level stare that he always gave her when he wasn't going to answer questions. "Believe what you want."

"Max," Tess said.

He shrugged. "She wanted a story. She doesn't have to have it. Do you still have your phone, Liz? We need to call the cops."

"Right here," Liz said, patting her purse, but not taking it out.

"Wait," Nila said. "What story?"

"I'll show you." Max started down the road, then paused. "But before we go too far, I need a promise from you."

"What's that?" Nila asked.

"First," he said, "you'll wait until we're gone before calling the police. When they get here, you won't mention any of us. Not me, Michael, Liz or Tess. You took care of these guys. We didn't. You got that?"

"The police aren't going to believe that," Nila said.

"That's not my problem," Max said. "Because if you don't agree to my terms, I'm setting the guys free, destroying the serum, and their files, and getting out of here."

"I thought you just told Liz to call the cops," Nila said.

"I changed my mind." Max had a low, calm way of speaking that conveyed a sense of utter conviction. "I can't trust you. And if I can't trust you, I can't trust that you'll keep our names out of this."

"You'd let criminals go free because of that?" Nila asked.

"Yes," Max said.

Nila sighed. This boy, this young man, this *powerful* young man, had her over a barrel every time she turned around. "All right. What else?"

"You won't mention us in connection to the Phoenix hospital and the December twenty-fourth event."

Event. He didn't call it a miracle; he called it an event. "I already made that promise," she said.

"No," he said. "You said you wouldn't give us to the police and you said you wouldn't mention our names. I don't want you to mention us at all."

"You're part of it," she said. "You and your friend Michael are known to the police. People know that you went into that room and that you disappeared from there."

"And that's all they need to know."

"All right," she said. "But I'd like to know. I think you owe me that."

"For what?" he asked. "Taking us across state lines? Three underage kids whom you just met this morning?"

"What?" Her eyes widened.

He gave her a small smile. "Those are the facts, Ms.

Spence. You drove three underage kids across state lines today. That you did it for a good reason doesn't change the fact that you did it without talking to our parents, and without legal permission. Think of what a person in command of those facts could do with them. You would look pretty bad."

"Why would you do that to me?"

"I didn't say I would," he said. "Any more than you said you'd misuse the facts about the Phoenix hospital. But just by putting those facts out there, there's the risk of misinterpretation. Don't you agree?"

"You're afraid I'll use whatever you tell me in the article?" she asked.

"After the article's in print, what recourse would I have?"

"You have to trust me at some point."

Max's small smile grew. "I do trust you. I came with you. I brought my friends. We will give you a story, if you want, one that, I think, will make a difference. Isn't that enough?"

Where did this kid get his composure? She'd talked to high-level, white-collar criminals who didn't have Max's smarts or his guts. And she'd talked to politicians who would kill for Max's negotiating skills and his inventiveness.

"Well?" Max asked.

"Deal," she said. "Although I'm still not sure how you boxed me into this position."

"You boxed yourself, Ms. Spence," he said as he headed to the car. And she knew it was true. Never once did she have the upper hand in any of this. She always wanted information from Max. He didn't claim to want anything from her.

Until now.

And he'd had enough time to prepare for that, so even if she had objections, he still had the upper hand.

Max got into the car.

So did Tess and Liz.

It took Nila a moment to realize she was supposed to drive them down the driveway.

21

March 25—Florence Junction, Arizona

Max sat rigidly in the front seat of the car. His heart was pounding. Nila Spence had agreed to all of his terms. He hadn't expected her to. He had thought there was a good possibility that he would have to hold her, then leave without giving her those guys, and then have to contact the police anonymously.

He was glad that hadn't happened. This would be easier, by a long shot.

Nila was driving down the dirt road, her eyes wide, as if she'd never seen it before. He wondered what kind of image Tess had given her when she'd actually stood on the road earlier. He had thought it strange that Nila accepted his explanation of sleep so readily.

Apparently, Tess had done better than he had thought she would. He had told her that he thought they would have to lie to Nila and make her think she'd been asleep. Apparently, Tess had messed with things just enough so that Nila believed everything she had "seen" in the last few hours had been a dream.

Thank heavens she had been so easy to convince. Max had actually expected to have a tougher time of it.

But, as he was beginning to learn, people usually accepted the mundane explanations of things. If something extraordinary happened in front of them, they were unwilling to believe it. They didn't want to know that aliens really existed, that their perceptions of reality could be altered, that the world wasn't always the way it seemed.

He guessed reporters were probably more vulnerable to that than most folks. Investigative reporters, like Nila Spence, saw the gritty underside of things. To learn that fantastic things were possible would probably mess with the grim realities of her life. She had to be able to see those things clearly to survive.

Anything else would be merely details.

She pulled the car up behind the truck. The house looked different with all of the lights on. It would have looked welcoming if it weren't for the open front door and the two men tied up in the entryway.

"Oh, Max," Liz said. "I didn't even ask if you were all right."

"Of course he's fine," Tess said.

"I'm fine," Max said as if Tess hadn't spoken. Sometimes her proprietary attitude toward him irritated him, especially when it was directed toward Liz.

Nila got out of the car. So did Max. He could see Michael through the window. He was standing near the tied-up men. Michael had straightened the guy's clearly broken leg to make them look less pounded.

Good job, Max thought. That way Nila wouldn't know they had even touched the computer. But he would have to make sure Michael had the disk he had been saving.

Liz and Tess got out, too. Liz was standing right behind him. "Can you tell me what was in that serum they were making?"

"Not without a lab," she said.

"Just a guess is all we need, I think."

"I'll have someone test the stuff," Nila said.

"I doubt I'll read your story," Max said to her, and started up the stairs and into the house.

Nila followed.

So did Tess and Liz.

Michael stepped forward as they approached.

"Any troubles?" Max asked.

"Sleeping like babies," Michael said. He stared at Nila. "So you're the famous reporter."

"And you're the missing Michael."

Max noticed that she was small next to him, but she looked really tough.

"Your friends were really worried about you today," she said.

He gave her a sardonic smile. "I'm sure that attracted you like blood attracts a shark."

"Michael!" Liz said.

He looked at her for the first time. "I thought you were worried about me."

"I was." She went over to him and hugged him. "Just don't mess with a reporter."

She said that loudly enough for everyone to hear. Nila

gave a rueful laugh. "I'm glad someone around here respects me."

"If I didn't respect you," Max said, "I wouldn't have brought you down here."

"Point taken." Nila stared at the entire room, taking a few extra moments to stare at the two men. "I'm going to need my camera."

"After we leave," Tess said.

"The serum," Max said to Liz.

"All the stuff is in the kitchen," Michael said.

Liz nodded and headed in that direction.

"Careful to not leave any fingerprints on anything," Max said. He glanced at Nila and Tess to make sure they understood as well.

Nila hadn't moved since she entered the room. "Somehow, I would have thought this place would have been more torn up. That guy down there is big. And you two don't look like you'd do well on *WWF Smackdown*."

Michael rolled his eyes.

Max shrugged, giving it a moment's thought on how to answer that. Finally he just said, "Sometimes you get lucky."

"With them having guns?" she asked, pointing at the gun still under the table.

Max said nothing. The less he said, the better they would all be.

Tess shook her head and walked out to the porch. Max understood. She didn't want to stay because she was afraid of what she might say.

Max nodded toward the computer. "You told me they did everything by e-mail. I'm assuming that's your gold mine. The money is hidden in the hallway. I hope you and the police will get it back to the rightful owners."

He glanced at Michael and he patted his pocket where the disk would be. Good.

"I'll make sure it happens," Nila said. "Was there any serum left in that kitchen? It would be good to have some."

"I don't think we should mess with this stuff too much," Max said. "We want the police to be able to make a complete case."

"There's serum in my car," Michael said. "I'll give it to you before we leave."

Max looked at him in surprise. Michael shrugged. "What am I supposed to do with it?"

"How did you get it?" Nila asked.

"That's a question you shouldn't ask," Max said before Michael could answer.

At that moment, Liz came out of the kitchen. Her eyes were dark coals in her face and her mouth formed a thin line. "Cough syrup and sugar water," she said.

"Are you sure?" Max asked.

"There wasn't anything else in there." Liz's cheeks were flushed too. She was as angry as he'd ever seen her. "Bottles of the stuff, all different. They mixed the cough syrups and gave it to sick children."

"That's bad, right?" Michael asked. "I had a hunch that whatever they were doing was bad for the kids."

"It was worse than if they'd just done sugar water," Liz said, her voice barely containing the anger.

"How much worse?" Max asked. He had to know.

"Have you ever read the warning label on cough syrup?" she asked. "Don't use it if you're pregnant, or have heart disease, or high blood pressure or diabetes. And all cough syrups have different ingredients. Drugs interact with each other. Who knows what this stuff was doing? It certainly wasn't harmless, even if it had been taken by a healthy adult. I don't want to think about what it did to sick children."

Max's stomach cramped up. That was exactly what he didn't want to hear.

Liz stopped in front of the two men, still unconscious on the floor. For a moment, Max thought she was going to kick them, but she didn't. He wouldn't have blamed her if she had. Finally she just sort of growled at them, and then went outside to join Tess.

"I don't like this, Michael," Max said.

"We stopped them," Michael said.

"But was it too late?"

Michael looked off into the distance. "I don't know," he said softly. "I hope not."

Max stared at him for a moment, wondering what really had happened in the last twenty-four hours. But he knew that Michael wouldn't tell him as long as the reporter was around.

"I think we should get out of here," Max said.

Michael nodded. He joined the girls outside on the porch. Max walked over to Nila. She had shut off the screen saver and was staring at the computer's menu.

"We have a deal?" he asked again.

"Yes," she said, not looking at him.

"All right." He reached into his pocket and handed her her phone. Tess had taken it from her earlier and had given it to him.

She stared at the phone like it was a snake.

"I don't know how long it'll take the police to get here, but I suspect it might be a while. Those guys are well tied up and Michael and I took their guns away from them. But you don't want to be alone when they wake up. They probably won't be the most agreeable company."

He knew for a fact they were going to be in a lot of pain. But he didn't mention that to her.

Nila pulled her gaze away from the phone in her hand to look at the tied-up men. She took a deep breath. Before she turned the phone on, she looked up at Max.

"You'd better get out of here before I call. It would be just our luck to have the police respond instantly."

Max smiled at her. "Michael will leave the serum on the turn-out."

"All right," she said. Then she extended her hand. "Nice doing business with you, Mr. Evans."

He took her hand. Her grip was firm, her expression filled with respect. "Likewise, Ms. Spence."

Then he joined his friends on the porch. As the four of them walked up the dirt road toward Michael's car, Max noted that a thread of light lined the eastern horizon.

It was dawn. Time to leave.

22

March 25—
Outside of Florence Junction, Arizona

Sometimes Liz didn't understand Tess. As they got into the car Michael had parked on the shoulder, Tess got into the passenger seat, so that she was sitting beside Michael. Liz had said that she should sit in back with Max, and Tess had nodded her head Yes.

"You should," she had said, and then settled in front.

Max didn't seem to notice any of it. He sat in the backseat and stared out the window as Michael headed the car up the road toward Tucson and told them what had happened to him.

As Michael talked, answering a few questions, Max just sat beside Liz, turning a computer disk Michael had given him over and over in his hand. Michael occasionally looked into the rearview mirror and frowned.

"What are you going to do with that disk, Maxwell?" he finally asked.

"Insurance," Max said.

Liz frowned, not at all certain about what was happening. "What's on the disk?"

"The names of all the families who were scammed," Michael said.

Liz felt her breath catch. She remembered the look on Max's face when he told her about saving Sydney, about the way he couldn't just abandon all those other sick children.

"What kind of insurance?" Tess asked. "In case Nila Spence doesn't live up to her side of the bargain?"

"Yeah," Max said, but Liz wasn't convinced by his tone. "I'll send this anonymously to the police if I have to. Those guys need to go away for life."

"They will," Michael said with such fury that Liz didn't doubt it.

Liz knew that without a doubt, if the police didn't put them away, Michael would do whatever needed to be done. He was that angry.

They drove for a while in silence. Max continued to stare out the window. As they passed through a small town, the store lights illuminated his face.

Liz recognized the expression. It was the same one he'd had when he had come to her window on Christmas Eve and told her about the children.

She slipped her hand through his. He looked at her in surprise.

"You can't do it, you know," she said, keeping her voice soft and as comforting as she could.

Tess looked at them over the car seat and, to Liz's surprise, smiled. Was this what Tess wanted? Someone to make sure that Max wouldn't do anything stupid?

"It's my fault," Max said. "None of these kids would be in this situation if I hadn't gone to the hospital in Phoenix that night and the press hadn't called it a miracle."

"No, Max," Liz said, "that's wrong."

Michael glanced into the rearview mirror this time, and Liz thought she saw relief on his face. He seemed to be worried about Max doing something, too.

As if Michael had the right to worry. He was taking Max to a hospital in Tucson to save the life of a little girl. It was December twenty-fourth all over again.

Only this time, Tess said she'd make sure no one knew they were there and no one remembered them.

Liz could only hope that Tess's powers weren't drained by her time spent controlling Nila Spence.

"It's not wrong, Liz," Max said. "It's what I have to do."

Liz shook her head and focused on Max. "No, I mean your assumption is wrong."

He looked down at their hands, clasped on the car seat.

"It's not your fault that these children are ill. They were ill when the parents contacted the scam artists. The medicine might have made them worse, but all the parents had to do was take them back to the hospital with a sample. The doctors would know what to do."

"But that's why the parents went to these guys in the first place," Max said. "Because they thought the hospitals weren't helping."

Liz sighed. "Sometimes no matter what we do, no matter how many powers we have, people die, Max."

He gripped her hand hard. "I won't let that happen. Not to anyone I care about."

She put her free hand over their clasped hands. "You might not have a choice."

He looked at her.

"Remember what I said to you on Christmas Eve?"

He nodded and looked away. "I can't believe that innocent children getting ill is part of some benevolent god's plan."

"I don't think you were placed here to perform miracles, Max," Liz said. "Think of what would happen if the word got out? You handled Nila Spence, but she had ethics. Imagine reporters who don't."

Max winced.

"And think of all the people who would claim they knew you or could do what you did? These men took advantage of your good deed. If you did a hundred more things like this, imagine what would happen then."

Max shook his head. "I can't think about what other people will do. I'm only responsible for what I do, Liz."

She nodded. "I know that. But sometimes you have to trust that the system will work. We're on the verge of a revolution in medicine, Max. You have no idea how sick these kids are. Maybe, even as we speak, some doctor is making them well."

Max's eyes were dark, haunted. "I'll never forget that night, Liz. I couldn't just leave them."

"You're not," she said. "You're not leaving any of these children, either. The police and Nila Spence will get to the parents. They'll get treatment if the serum made them sicker, and they'll probably get their kids the right kind of help because of it. It'll probably scare them enough that they'll never try something this risky again."

Max sighed. "I know you're right."

"You need to rest," Liz said. "There is one little girl that you are going to help, and she's not too far from here. You want to be at your best."

"Yeah," Max said softly. He closed his eyes and leaned his head back.

In the front seat Michael nodded and Tess let out a slight sigh.

Liz watched Max for a moment, praying that the little girl whose father had kidnapped Michael, the little girl who had ridden in the backseat of this very car, had a room all to herself.

Because the one thing Liz didn't say to Max—the thing none of them could say to Max—was how scared they had all been at the way he had drained his powers that night.

She didn't want him to do that again.

March 25—Somewhere between Bensen and Tucson, Arizona

"Okay," Maria said as she set her purse on the car seat beside her. "Does someone want to tell me the point of spending the night outside a diner called Pie 'N' Stuff? Why didn't Michael just tell us to meet him in Tucson in the first place?"

"You should have asked him," Isabel said. She was in the backseat, her head back, eyes closed. She sounded exhausted.

"I did ask him," Maria said. "Didn't you hear me ask him? He said it would all be clear when we get there. Does that make any sense to any of you?"

"Am I the only one who's concerned that we're meeting all four of them at a hospital?" Valenti said.

He was driving as casually as he had before, one hand on the wheel, the other on the stick. But Maria noticed that his speed was a notch or two higher than it should have been.

"He sounded fine, didn't he?" Alex said.

"Max is with him." Isabel still hadn't opened her eyes. "I'm not worried now."

Neither was Maria. But now that the worry was gone, irritation had taken its place. Michael had led them on some weird wild goose chase, and he hadn't explained any of it—yet.

"I'm cold and I'm tired, and we didn't even have breakfast," she said.

"I offered to buy you something at four A.M.," Alex said patiently. "You said you weren't hungry."

"I was *worried*," Maria said. "How can anyone eat when they're worried?"

"Alex did," Isabel said.

"I wasn't the only one. You both did, too." Alex looked from her to Valenti.

"*I* didn't," Maria said.

"We can stop and get something," Valenti said.

"No." Maria crossed her arms. "If we miss him again, he might make us go to the Grand Canyon or something. Maybe this is just one big game to him."

"I doubt it," Alex said.

"Why do you men always stick together?" Maria asked him.

"Don't answer that," Valenti said.

"See?" Maria looked at Isabel. "They're doing it now."

"No, they're not," Isabel said. "Because I'm with them. Just relax, Maria. He's fine."

"He's fine. You're all so certain he's fine." She flounced back in her seat and looked at the mile markers. Only one mile since the last time she looked.

This trip was going to take forever—which was probably a good thing, since she had to figure out what kind of reaction she'd have when she saw Michael.

She would want to hug him, but she wasn't sure he deserved a hug. After all, he'd stood her up, forgotten to call her, made her drive to Nowhere, Arizona, without explanation, and then made her wait all night.

On the other hand, he'd called as soon as he could, and he had called her, not Max. And he had a good excuse for standing her up. Maybe he even had a good excuse for not meeting her in Nowhere, Arizona.

She would have to wait and see.

She shook her head. Michael. He was really the most exasperating person she knew.

Which was one of the things that made him so very interesting—and attractive.

A hug. She smiled. Definitely a hug first. Then she'd react, depending.

She settled back in her seat, feeling better now that she had her reaction all planned.

March 25—Tucson, Arizona

The hospital was very quiet. It wasn't even five A.M., although it seemed a lot later. The sun had just crept over the horizon, but it had been lighting the sky for some time now.

Michael hadn't realized how exhausted he was until he went to the emergency room and found one of the night nurses.

"Katie Newcomb," he'd asked. "I'm her brother."

"She's upstairs," the nurse had said, and had given him a room number.

So now he, Max, Liz, and Tess were walking down the corridor as if they belonged there. No nurse stopped them, and no one noticed them.

This time, he was very aware of the hospital security camera. Tess couldn't do anything about that, but he might be able to—if he had to.

If someone was in Katie's room. If people figured out there was a miracle.

Michael could tell that Liz didn't think this was a good idea. He didn't either, but he had no other choice. That little girl had nearly died because of him. And for all the pretty speeches that Liz had given Max, Max really was right. It didn't matter once you saw the child's face.

From that point on, you did everything you could to save her.

Fortunately, Max understood that. When Michael had told him what he wanted him to do, Max hadn't hesitated.

They arrived at Katie's room. It was a private room with a large Bugs Bunny painted on the door. Through the small window Michael could see Chad Newcomb sitting in the chair beside the bed.

Michael let out a small sigh. At least Katie was still alive. He'd been terrified that they lost her during the night.

He and Max had agreed that the three would wait outside the room while Michael found out what was going on. Maybe Michael could even get Newcomb to leave.

He braced himself, then pushed open the door. Newcomb looked up.

"How is she?" Michael asked.

The smile on Newcomb's face as he stood was like nothing Michael had ever seen. "She's going to be fine. They finally found out what was wrong."

Michael stared.

Newcomb went on, his smile growing. "She had a very rare virus that attacks the heart. It's very rare in children. Maybe one case in a million. But this emergency room doctor had interned with some specialist on it, and recognized it. No one thought to test for it. He doubted anyone had ever seen a case like it in Arizona."

Michael's head spun. He was tired. He wasn't sure what Newcomb was saying. "So she's going to recover?"

"She'll need attention for a few more days, but yes, she will. Thanks to you forcing me to come here."

The words rocked Michael. "What?"

Newcomb stood and reached out his hand. "I hope you will forgive me for hitting you and taking you from your home. I was desperate and stupid."

Michael stared at Newcomb's hand. After a moment, he took it. Michael was beginning to understand the desperation that motivated the man.

"Katie is going to be all right," Michael said. "That's all that's important."

"You have every right to have me arrested," Newcomb said, staring into Michael's eyes.

"I won't mention a word of it," Michael said, "if you don't mention me when the police contact you about the Internet fraud and me borrowing your car for a few hours. Those guys are out of business now, and it looks like you're going to get your money back."

Newcomb smiled. "I'd have spent every nickel I had for this night to happen. I don't know how you did it, but you have a deal."

Michael then reached into his pocket and handed Newcomb the car keys. Newcomb stared at them for a moment, as if they were a reminder of his stupidity.

Finally, he brightened. "You want to see Katie?"

"Yeah," Michael said.

Both he and Newcomb moved to the side of the bed. Katie was asleep, as she had been most of the time he had been with her. Tubes covered her arms, and a monitor was attached to her chest.

Yet even with all the equipment, she looked better. Her skin color was almost normal, and she didn't seem as frail as she had just a few hours before.

"She's beautiful," Michael said.

Newcomb smiled. "She looks like her mother. For a while, I thought I'd lost both of them."

Michael thought about Maria, and how it would feel to lose her. Then he shook his head. Maybe he hadn't completely understood Newcomb's desperation, after all.

"Mind if I stay here for a few minutes?" Michael asked.

"Not at all," Newcomb said. "After all, you saved her life."

Without using his powers.

Without doing anything except the right thing.

He'd finally gotten his wish.

He'd finally been able to help someone without relying on Max.

Without relying on anyone but himself.

Michael looked down at Katie, who was going to be just fine, and realized he had never felt better in his life.